TWENTY
TWENTY

TWENTY TWENTY

ANURAAG SRIVASTAVA

Srishti
PUBLISHERS & DISTRIBUTORS

Srishti Publishers & Distributors
Registered Office: N-16, C.R. Park
New Delhi – 110 019
Corporate Office: 212A, Peacock Lane
Shahpur Jat, New Delhi – 110 049
editorial@srishtipublishers.com

First published by
Srishti Publishers & Distributors in 2017

The Years Before

It was a beautiful, breezy evening for the party by the sprawling pool. Music wafted melodiously as guests engaged in animated conversations. Excitement was in the air with well dressed technocrats of both sexes discussing the latest in technology. Some among them were glued to the Twenty20 match going on between Delhi Daredevils and Mumbai Indians on the large screen placed near the bar counter. It was an after party, part of a symposium held for technocrats from across the country to deliberate on the technological advancements in the field of software development. It was a stage to showcase the achievements in technology by some software companies, while others were keen to learn some new techniques. This was a good platform for software company officials to explore collaborations and also identify possible assets they could poach.

Sitting on a separate table with three of his contemporaries, all owners of different companies, Uday seemed quite jubilant. It had been a long time since the old school-mates had met. Though Uday had somehow raced ahead of them in terms of the turnover his company churns in comparison to theirs, their friendship was beyond business relations. Remembering their earlier days of struggle, they were totally oblivious of the other guests. Uday was rather silent, perhaps concentrating on something important with his eyes focussed on his glass of vodka. The group near the television screen was now more vocal as the match was nearing to a close finish. The dance floor was slowly coming alive as the drinks made their way to some shy minds. Smooch-faced selfies were being taken while some photographer was clicking photos for the page 3 editions. Common scenes in party circles in Delhi. Uday excused himself, came out of the venue to check on someone and then giving some instructions to his driver, went back to his table ordering one more drink. The drinks flowed, the music thumped, the lights flashed and the party continued.

The Days Here

Abright sunny morning with a cool breeze instantly makes
the north Indian summer pleasant. By ten in the morning,
all offices are usually bustling with activity, giving a good start to
the day ahead. Most of the screens on desktops and laptops are
waiting for the morning bell of the stock market. Since January,
markets had been nose-diving to a new low every day with a
hope that the next day it may rise a little. But the next day it
again touched its lowest. Many financial institutions defaulted
and the markets taking the brunt had resulted in a rippling effect
on many.

Abhimanyu had all his senses concentrated on the screen
in front of his eyes. The eyes checking the figures, the fingers
on the keyboard, the ears plugged with his Bluetooth set and
mouth speaking continuously while checking out the latest
news. His portfolio had not been large in terms of volume, but
diverse up to a greater extent. He had tried to distribute his risk
between different sectors: cement, metal, telecom, banking, and
infrastructure. Though he had about two years of experience
in stock investing, but those two years had been exceptional in
giving good results, while these last few months had demolished
all notions of experience and expertise in the market. The only

exit route visible was to become a spectator rather than a player. The losses had created a record of negative figures. More infusion was only adding up to more losses. Averaging was minimal as stocks were battered to new lows every day.

Abhi, as Abhimanyu was called, also entered the market with a new hope every day and finished the day with some more red figures in his portfolio. It has been five years since he had started his job after graduating from an engineering college in Bangalore and had joined the IT industry during its boom time. A high salary and comfortable working hours made the package attractive. Since then, he had given his best to the company and earned a lot in performance bonuses, along with hefty increments. Higher earning created a higher urge for expenditure too. Moreover, higher purchasing power brings with it the flamboyancy of brand power. An expensive branded wardrobe, LCD television, high end bikes, and personal accessories. A little expense on oneself inflated credit card bills expecting to be cleared by next month's salary. While it so happened for the first couple of years, after that, when the salary was not sufficient, the purchasing power got artificially inflated by the number of figures in enhanced credit card limits. By the third year, Abhi's salary was just enough to revolve the limits on his cards.

Abhi always thought whatever he bought was just a little expense on himself which was compensated by the feeling of the high he achieved while showcasing his possessions to the world. His life revolved around shopping malls, discotheques, bars, food plazas and his office. Family was never a priority; his parents were far off in a village, living happily on the land produce and a small pension. His sister was well off, working at an IT institute and earning handsomely. Though Abhi and her sister shared the apartment and were very fond of each other, they rarely talked to each other except on the dining table. Their individual rooms became individual spaces. The kitchen and the dining area were the only meeting places for them. Sunday and other holidays were usually spent outside their apartment with their respective friends.

Abhi was enjoying life to the fullest. The yearly increments of his salary were coming in. Credits were running smoothly, and markets were continuously being flooded with latest articles which Abhi always wanted to purchase. It was just like that day in the summers of the year two years back that Shashank had introduced him to the dynamics of the stock market. Shashank's younger brother had just joined as a sales executive with a share trading company and he had got Abhi's trading account opened. It was fun to invest in a large corporate from the easy comfort of your home or office, without having to feel the heat of the market floor. As trained by Shashank, Abhi started investing in the secondary market for a minimal amount from one thousand to five thousand bucks. With little amount invested and markets giving good returns, the addition in share values gave enough motivation to invest more.

Though profits, vis-a-vis the amount invested, was good in terms of percentage, but the profit in terms of money was itself meagre. If only he had invested larger amounts, the profits would have mattered. Abhi was intelligent enough to first spend some time analyzing the stock market and studying the trends of specific target companies. He selected a few companies which had lower chances of going below his purchase price. During this period, he also used to visit a broking company to understand the dynamics of the market. Abhi prepared himself to a good degree in order to take a big plunge into the market. Abhi believed money attracts money, hence he needed to invest big money to get greater returns. He wanted to clear all his credit card dues in a single shot. He tried to apply for a loan, but being on the list of higher end credit card borrowers, the financial institutions were not ready to take any more risks.

One evening with Shashank and Anubhav, they started discussing the rise of the market over beer. Anubhav was specifically enthusiastic about the stocks he had acquired which were giving exceptionally good returns. It was during this session that Anubhav told everyone about his trip to Manali where he had met his dream girl and had decided to settle down with her. But Abhi seemed more interested in the shares which were giving such high returns and cursing himself for not having enough money to be put in.

"How much do you think would be a good investment, at present?"asked Shashank.

"It should be somewhere between twenty to thirty lakhs which will ensure enough profits in six months to enable us to have a credit free life!" exclaimed Abhi.

◆

It was around one week later, that Shashank introduced him to Raghubir, who was into the business of wholesale trade and also lent money on a little higher interest than the banks. Abhi got a loan of twenty lakhs from him on the personal guarantee of Shashank, though Raghubir never insisted on any guarantee; he had more confidence in his own ways of recovering a loan. As per the arrangement, Abhi had to give two percent interest per month and was to return the full principal after one year. It was a very good arrangement for Abhi and was extremely thankful to Shashank for getting this amount arranged. By the next week, Abhi had all twenty lakhs invested into high grade stocks and was starting to make interesting profits.

But it was all six months back, and now when Abhi is refreshing his computer screen to get the latest quotes, every such refresh is costing him some more bucks. An investment of twenty lakhs six months back has dropped down to a meagre three lakhs on his portfolio and he had still to pay the two percent interest on the twenty lakhs loan to Raghubir. He knew by now that he had lost all the money in the market and was not in a position to pay the interest amount too. Presently, he was more worried about the interest amount rather than the money lost. Being aware of the ways resorted by men like Raghubir to recover their money, he somehow ensured to pay the interest amount. Selling the shares at this point was more fatal and he had to wait for the market to spring back. But the global cues seemed to put this event at a farther end. The due date for the interest amount was coming near and so was the due date of all his credit card dues. Abhi toggled back to his company's working screen. The day's work had begun.

✦

Business was not good in the commodity market, prices were not rising and the demand was flat. Though Raghubir had stocked a lot in his godown, he was still not getting a good price. He had lost some money in share trading, but was not concerned. His main concern revolved around his commodity trading business. His people were busy with phone calls finalising other deals, while he was dealing with his customers, all traders from his community, taking stock of rise and fall of prices. Not even once did it cross his mind that he had to collect interest from different borrowers. He had approximately three hundred million rupees lent out to different borrowers, but he was not concerned. It was just a small amount he had invested, that too for the sake of earning out of some idle money lying around.

As he was busy bargaining with his customers, his mobile phone rang, it was on his personal number, "Yes, boss ... But boss, it's only the interest portion ... But there is still some time left ... Okay, as you say ... How can I question you?" he conversed timidly.

Raghubir remained bewildered after the call was disconnected and more surprised over the instruction he had received. Though he was an independent businessman and quite a muscleman himself, he could not let his men see him talking meekly to someone. He usually got little sweat droplets on his forehead after a call from him. It was always something important and he needed to come out of his comfort zone to get the job done. He was the boss, after all.

Raghubir called Bholu in the evening, his confidante, and told him to get his men along as some recovery had to be done. For Bholu it was a usual job as he had been working for Raghubhai for years. In times of need, whenever he got embroiled in some police mess, it was Raghubhai who bailed him out. Raghubhai was his godfather and he was always ready to execute any job for him.

Bholu was in Raghu's office with three of his men in the evening. Nothing happens without a reason, but this time, Bholu was not able to reason out the instructions given to him. Raghubhai didn't tell him why, but just told him to do his bidding. Bholu has never seen him behave this impatiently. He took the slip with the address written on it.

It was nearly 11:00 p.m. when Bholu pressed the doorbell, accompanied by his three men showcasing their bulging muscles as they folded their hands across their chests. Aditi opened the door and astonished at the unusual guests asked, "Yes, whom do you want?"

"Is Abhimanyu there? Tell him Raghubhai sent ..."

"Abhi ..." Aditi shouted, "Your friends please ..." and went inside, leaving the door open.

Bholu stepped inside and stood there, taking a good look at Aditi while she went into her room. From the second door appeared Abhimanyu and recognising Bholu said, "Oh, you at this time? The date is tomorrow. I will pay the interest in the morning. Haven't withdrawn it from my account yet."

"Yeah, I know it's tomorrow, but Raghubhai sent me to inform you that tomorrow, along with the interest, he wants the full principal as well ..."

"What! Are you mad? How can I pay the principal now? There are six months left!"

"Hey you ... don't tell Raghubhai how much time is left. It's his money and he can take it back anytime."

"But he had given it to me for one year, how can he demand it before time?"

"Raghubhai gave you money on his terms, not yours. So better arrange it by tomorrow, I will come to your office."

"But how? I don't have the money at present."

"That's your problem. Don't make it our problem or it'll become a very big problem for you ... understood?" He threatened as he walked out of the door.

"But ... but ... how ... hey listen ..."

While Abhi tried to reason, Bholu and his men went down the staircase, out of sight.

"What does all this mean? Why sending the men at this hour and demanding all the money? I will talk to Raghubhai. It's a mistake. Raghu must have sent them for someone else," Abhi kept murmuring as he went back to his room. He tried to call Raghubhai, but the phone was switched off.

When Abhi woke up the next morning, the events of the night came back to him and he felt dismayed. He tried to call Raghubhai twice, but both times the phone was switched off. He got ready and left for his office, reminding himself to withdraw forty thousand from an ATM en route.

Bholu had informed Raghubhai in the night itself about his visit to Abhi's house. The development was communicated to the Boss by Raghubhai and in turn Raghubir got a fresh set of instructions. At around 11:00 a.m. Bholu came to meet Raghubir.

"So, bhai, the boy did not seem to believe his ears. Now I have to go to his office and collect how much? Twenty lakhs plus forty thousand, right?"

"No, just relax! At what time did you go yesterday?"

"At around eleven in the night."

"Then go to his house at around 11:30 tonight and ask him to pay immediately."

"And if he doesn't pay?"

"Give him a piece of your mind and one more day to arrange the money. But yes, do collect the interest."

"Okay bhai, that will be done. And yes, it's better to go to his house … he has a beautiful sister."

"Fine then, now go to Som seth. He has not paid interest for the last two months, see that he is not able to default in the future …"

"Okay, he will not think of defaulting ever again!" Saying that, Bholu left with his men.

✦

Abhi had forty thousand ready in his pocket, impatiently waiting for Bholu. But neither did Bholu come, nor could Abhi contact Raghubir. After packing up for the day, Abhi went straight to his flat, made some noodles and watched a movie on HBO with two beer cans. Aditi had gone to some friend's house to stay and would be returning a couple of days later.

It was around 11:30 and Abhi was getting ready to go to bed when the doorbell rang. As he opened the door Bholu, pushed himself in, shoving Abhi back.

"Hey, hey ... what is this? What are you doing here at this time? I waited all day at office."

"Money ... where is the money?" said Bholu, putting his right hand palm towards Abhi while his eyes searched the house.

"Yes, it was all ready in the morning itself. Have I ever defaulted? I will just bring it." Saying that, Abhi went to his room.

There were two more men with Bholu, one of them whispered, "She has gone to sleep so early?"

Abhi came back and handed twenty two-thousand rupee notes to Bholu. He counted them and said. "And the rest?"

"What rest? This is the interest I have to pay every month," said Abhi.

"Don't you keep your ears open? I came yesterday to tell you specifically that the full principal is also to be paid!" shouted Bholu.

"But I don't understand. It was given to me for one year, and six months are still left."

"I don't know all that. Raghubhai says full money ... now!"

"Let me talk to Raghubhai. I have been trying to reach him since yesterday, but his phone is switched off."

"You can talk to Raghubhai only when he wants you to talk to him. For now, talk to me. Where is the rest of his money?"

"But you don't understand, I don't have so much money."

"That's your problem, you make money, build money, whatever you do, just give me twenty lakhs more and I am a happy man. I will go, you go and sleep after that."

"But I don't have it now ..."

"I can give you maximum one day more. You arrange it, else, not only I will pick every straw from this house, but also sell all your bones to the highest bidder!" He turned away and they left.

Abhi kept looking at the door as they left murmuring abuses. Abhi was still in shock. He was a good boy, paying the interest at the right time. Why was this happening? With these thoughts, Abhi fell into a troubled sleep.

Bholu went straight to Raghu's house, handed him the money and briefed him. Twenty thousand was handed back to him. After Bholu left, Raghubir threw the rest of the notes into one of the wooden drawers, looked up at the moon through his window and went to make his bed.

Raghubhai usually wore white kurtas and white dhotis, wrapping a piece of cloth around his neck. He had been into the commodity trading business for a long time. Techniques of trading in spices, sugar and betel nut had been learnt just like his mother tongue. Since childhood, he had been carrying bags full of hard cash to banks or to his father's godown. The amount of cash in the godown was a hundred times more than what he used to deposit in banks. Trading settlements through bank accounts were done only for a very minimal amount. Most of the settlements were done in cash to avoid any government interference. Paying taxes was believed to be a foolish thing anyway. Raghubhai believed, the government should give an incentive to them as they helped trade to grow and helped to provide important usables to the general public.

Ironically it was Raghubhai who cursed the government for potholes on the roads. Who was going to tell him that it was because of people like him that development work in the nation suffered.

Amassing wealth had come naturally to Raghubhai and this had also developed anti government misconceptions. It seemed the laws of the land provided him with ways to go against them and he started having fun in doing exactly what the law prohibited. He was intelligent enough not to murder anyone or involve himself in any physical act directly; after all, lending money was one of his business activities to keep himself afloat in the market as a muscleman.

While he was a godfather to many, he himself had a godfather in business. He did small jobs for him, who in turn kept him safe. Raghu had never involved himself in any extortion or smuggling activities. He was satisfied only with lending money for personal benefit or placing money into different transactions to stay close to some top bureaucratic officials. Raghu was quite satisfied with all his activities. He had largely established himself as a white collar citizen of India, who on the one hand was living a middleclass businessman's life, and on the other hand was getting immense job satisfaction in doing all other types of adventurous jobs.

The next morning, Raghu called Bholu inquiring about Som seth and was quite satisfied with what Bholu told him. Raghu never allowed any of his men to carry any firearms or sharp objects while going for an expected heated appointment. Blood made him sweat. All through these years of handling people had made him more of a psychiatrist. He could read their minds and knew exactly what to do and when. He had expertise in creating mental pressure and the fear of the unknown.

He called up Bholu to inquire about Abhi's sister, whether she had been present during their second encounter. "No, I think she was out. We made quite a noise, but she didn't even peep out," said Bholu.

"Okay, don't talk to Abhi now, I will tell you what and when."

Raghu again took his cell phone and dialled. "Hi ... Shashank how are you? Just called you up to check if there are any persons who need money ... well come on, let's have a drink ... today evening ... that does fine ... see you then."

He looked at his watch, smiled a bit and went to his bathroom to change and leave for his office cum shop. It was a new day.

In the evening, Raghu had a meeting with Shashank where he inquired about Abhi and his sister. He was satisfied with the information he got. After the meeting, he again called Bholu and asked him to position two of his men to keep a watch on Abhi's house.

Bholu kept apprising him of the observations of his men as and when he got any information. On Monday evening, when Bholu informed him that Abhi's sister had come, Raghu immediately asked Bholu to come to him with four of his men and to remove the two men from the watch at Abhi's house.

Aditi had come back on Monday morning but had gone straight to her office. It was a long day after two seemingly very short days of the exciting weekend. For the whole day, she only asked her students to make a programme and test it on their systems, with little interference from her side. She had spent the last two days with Kajal and her friends at a resort off the Gurgaon-Jaipur highway. It was a cool place with water pools for different water sports, indoor gaming facilities, a discotheque with bar and a relaxing spa. Kajal's friend Vibhor was showing a lot of interest in her, but she was used to such attention. She tried to give little attention to Vibhor's efforts to get close to her and kept her guard up.

Aditi smiled while thinking about how Vibhor had tried to stay close to her and how several times he got himself involved in group conversations to get a direct response from her. But Aditi praised herself for staying aloof. Most boys just need a little encouragement and they'd waste no time in getting close. For them, nothing but a physical relation matters. Being in a physical relation was fine, but only when both were comfortable. Aditi had not had the experience yet, but the thought of it excited her. There was another reason she did not give Vibhor a chance to come close, and that was her fear of the past events in her life. She feared boys who flaunt money and have freedom to use it as they please.

The rich boy syndrome had entered her mind only after the incident with Rajal. It was two years back that she had met Rajal during a seminar she was attending on 'New Opportunities for the Information Technology Sector' at New Delhi. During the lunch break, they met while they reached for the rice at the same time. She was filling in for her Centre Director, while Rajal was there to understand the use of the knowledge he had gained through his studies. Rajal was a nice chap with boyish charm. They again met in the evening. Though they did meet on a happy note, it was the last meeting they had. Aditi was very excited that evening when she went to meet Rajal and had butterflies in her stomach. After all, Rajal had all the physical and mental qualities she had always dreamt of in her partner. And like a normal girl of her age going to have her first date, she had already started dreaming of an exotic future ahead.

That evening, everything went well: the hotel, the ambience, the food and the conversation they had. But it seemed too good to be true. Some time into the evening, Rajal asked her if they could spend the night together.

"What!" exclaimed Aditi, not able to believe her ears. "No way … what do you think of me? We have just met, it's only the second meeting today."

"So what! I am just asking us to extend this very beautiful and enjoyable evening till early morning and we can have a really good time in my lavish bed."

Aditi, in a fit of rage, just took her bag, got up and ran towards the exit. She could still remember Rajal coming up and catching up with her near the gate. She had tears in her eyes as Rajal spoke, "Well darling, I want to have you tonight. If you want, I can pay you in lakhs … whatever you want. You make my night and I promise will make your life …"

Aditi freed herself from Rajal's clutches and ran away to get into a taxi as soon as possible.

Aditi's eyes became moist while thinking of that encounter. She could still remember Rajal for both good and bad reasons. Every time she came across people behaving like Vibhor, she remembered Rajal and bitterness ran through her body. She was not averse to having a relationship with the opposite sex, but remained careful of penetrating eyes looking out for a whore in every woman.

That evening, after finishing her job, Aditi went straight to her house. Abhi was still not back; she changed her clothes and went to the kitchen to make something for dinner. By ten, Abhi was back. They both greeted each other and for the next half an hour or so, both caught up with what was the latest with the other.

As they retired to their respective rooms, the doorbell rang. Abhi got suspicious and came running from his room and reached the main door before Aditi could get up from her bed. As he opened the door, Bholu pushed himself in and made way for Raghubhai to enter, followed by two other men.

"How are you Abhi seth? Everything fine?" Raghubhai.

"Yes bhai, everything fine. Why did you take the pain to come? You could have called me," said Abhi, feeling relaxed seeing Raghubhai smiled.

"You wanted to talk to me, so I thought I should meet you personally."

"Yes bhai, actually Bholu was pressing me for the principal amount while six months are still left, that is why I wanted to meet you. I think there is some misunderstanding."

"What misunderstanding? He was just following my orders," said Raghu very calmly.

"But bhai, how can I pay now? I don't have money right now. Please give me six months and I will arrange it."

"No no. I need it now or else I wouldn't have pressed for it."

"But bhai, try to understand. I need time."

"Abhi, I need my money urgently. I can't wait six months, but I am ready to give you some more time."

"Bhai, then give me at least two months."

"Two months!! Are you mad? You arrange it in one week or believe me, I will sell off each and every thing in your house, including you," Raghu shouted.

"How can I arrange it in one week? The money is invested in the stock market and nearly washed off. I need some more time to recover it from the market or arrange from somewhere else."

"Do you think I am a roadside vendor you are bargaining with? By the way, you have a beautiful sister ... ask her if she can arrange it in a week's time. It's easier for her, you know."

"Raghubhai!" shouted Abhi "You are crossing your limits."

"You don't understand, my boy," Raghu grabbed Abhi's neck with his left hand. "If I cross my limits, you are gonna be nowhere."

Raghu left Abhi's neck with a jerk. "Now listen to me very carefully," started Raghu in a commanding voice. "I am being generous enough to allow you twenty days. In twenty days, you arrange the money and pay me. After twenty days, I'll pick your beautiful sister here, and believe me, I can arrange people from whom your sister can earn more than this amount in only four or five days ..."

"Raghu, mind you language. I will kill you if you utter a single word about my sister," Abhi yelled, charging towards Raghu. Bholu came in between and held him back.

"You can't do a thing even if I go and rape your sister right now. But I am a gentleman, I give you twenty days. Or believe me, Bholu and I have already developed a liking for your sister," said Raghu smiling.

Abhi struggled to free himself from Bholu's hold "I will kill you both ..."

"Better think of arranging the money. Killing someone is not your arena, leave it to people like us. We are good at it," Raghu explained. "Come on Bholu, let's go! We will come after twenty days, either to pick a bag full of currency or a body full of beauty. Let Abhi decide. Good night and sweet dreams."

Raghu and his men went back through the door and down the stairs, leaving Abhi stunned in his living room. He closed the door and with a heavy heart moved towards his room. He glanced towards Aditi's room; it was closed and seemed dark. He went into his room, sat on the bed and burst into tears.

Aditi was sitting by her door in total darkness, listening to Abhi drag his feet towards his room and close the door. She started sobbing, putting her head between her knees. After what she had heard, she became more convinced that most men look for a whore in every woman.

1st Day

It was the second day of the week, but Abhi felt as if it was doomsday and the world would come to an end. Checking all the possibilities of accumulating twenty lakhs was futile as he would end up negative with more to pay, rather than to save. He slowly dragged himself out of the bed and went to the bathroom. All the freshening up activities together also could not bring the morning glow on his face. 'Tough days ahead' – the warning showed on his face. Abhi had to think of some way to either pay Raghubhai or disappear from the world along with Aditi, whichever would be easier. He had a large friend circle, but he wondered if they could be approached for financial help. But still, the first thing that came to his mind was to seek help from some of his friends.

He got ready and went to the kitchen; breakfast was on the table. This meant Aditi had already left.

"Thank God she has left, or she may have guessed something is wrong," Abhi murmured aloud. "Hope she didn't hear anything last night." Speaking to oneself gives a boost to the sagging morale and helps rebuild the heartbeat to its normal tune. Abhi sat down to have his breakfast and began to think of all possible options. Shashank may have it, but he had also lost money in the market. Rohit earned well, but had high expenses. Atul may spare some; Manav may not be able to give much. But if all his three friends did lend him some money, it would not total up to more than five lakhs.

If he takes on another job and works all night along with the present job, it would still be impossible to accumulate anywhere near a lakh in the next twenty days. Abhi went to his office, but all along the route, the churning within the mind continued. Many solutions seemed to come to his mind, but they all seemed impractical.

"What should I do? Can't God make the stock market reach the highest in its history in just one week! This is possible if all the bad debts get realised in the United States and the FIIs get flooded with enough liquidity so that they push money in the Indian market. With increase in FII inflow, the markets will rebound. All this should happen within this week itself. Oh God, help borrowers like me to repay their debts in a single shot to their creditors. Let all these banks who have gone bankrupt rise again from their ashes and stand up to their old glory. This is the only way to get the stock market gain and recover the money. I will just withdraw twenty lakhs and finish off with Raghu!

Why can't some bandits run across me being followed by the police, and some packets of cash slip out of their bags and fall into my hands? This is a rare possibility, but could happen in this city where somewhere someone is robbing and running every minute. But then, it is a matter of luck only, nothing sure.

Why don't I rob someone! It is difficult, but possible. So many white collared businessmen keep their black money stocked in godowns and other places. If I can get my hand on any of these, my problem will be solved. But how will I come to know which are these businessmen. Even if I come to know that they have hidden money in a particular godown, how will I break in? Even if I am able to break in and somehow get hold of some money, what if I get caught? The police will show no mercy. No, no. I can't do that. Think of something else, Abhi.

Aditi was looking at the screen, but was not trying to decipher anything appearing on it. Her grey cells were instead trying to figure out how she has landed in a situation which she had not created. It is said that a person is responsible for his own actions, but was she responsible for other's actions too? Maybe yes. Why should she be involved in a mess someone else has created? Why is it that a woman gets involved primarily because of her sexuality? A woman is only thought of as an object of desire. Why didn't that man ask my brother to check if his sister could lend some money from her savings, why was only her sexuality noticed? Were those guys pimps? And if so, how did my brother get involved with them? Has he taken a loan and guaranteed me against non-payment? Should I ask Abhi about it? He will have to explain now that I am also involved. If these goons are serious, then I am neck deep in it. And if they have already planned to pick me up … should I run away … but where? Let me first talk to Abhi and not jump on to conclusions. Let me take an informed step.

Aditi reached home, freshened up and waited for Abhi. She kept watching television and after waiting till 11:30, had her dinner and went to her room. She vaguely heard Abhi coming after she had gone to sleep.

Abhi returned home quite late, had his dinner and went to his room to rest his brain for a while. But even on his cosy bed, the mind refused to shut down. After an hour or so, Abhi sat up, went to the balcony, lit up a smoke and let his mind wander.

2nd Day

When Aditi woke up, it was around five in the morning.

If I talk to Abhi, he may feel embarrassed and will also not share the complete details. Now I already know that he requires twenty lakhs in the next twenty days. As far as I know, he does not have it, nor do I. Some arrangement has to be made, but how? she pondered.

None of her friends could lend her such a large amount. There seemed to be no way out. But wait, where the hell had Abhi spent so much money? He had neither bought an expensive luxury item, nor had he bought any immovable property. I can't understand why he needed so much money which has now got me in huge trouble without any fault of mine.

The people who were threatening Abhi seem to be the sorts who work with their biceps rather than their grey cells. I have an option of taking a restraining order in my favour, but then it would in no way alleviate the problems for Abhi. If there is an easy way to lose money, then there will also be an easy way to earn it. Life reciprocates in some way. But why is it that female sexuality comes in between, even if there are other ways, she said to herself.

Suddenly something clicked in Aditi's mind and she got up immediately. By 7:00 a.m. she was ready and went out to hail a taxi for her office.

Abhi heard the click of the door closing and got up from his bed. It had been a nearly sleepless night. They may not be serious about Aditi, but still, chances couldn't be taken. He should send Aditi to their parents in the village, he thought. She will be safe in the village and by that time if he can arrange the sum, he'd stay, or else run away to some other smaller city. Abhi got dressed for office and sat on the oval dining table to have the breakfast already laid out by Aditi. He was still thinking hard on how to arrange for the money. He planned to check all his bank balances and stocks and confirm how much liquid money he had in store. Once he was aware of the exact amount he already had, then he would have to see how that amount could be used to arrange for the rest. Later in the day, he calculated that he had about one and a half lakhs without having to liquidate his stock holdings, which was an additional two lakhs as on date. But what about the rest of the amount? All the items which he had – like furniture, air conditioner, television, refrigerator, etc. – would not amount to more than a lakh and a half. There were also no loan schemes except for housing renovation which he could avail for twenty lakhs by giving a margin of ten percent, but then he would need property papers. A personal loan was out of the question with the number of EMIs deducted from his account.

What if he buys some spurious items from the grey market and sells them at a premium in some low society areas or nearby villages? There was a market at Delhi where a variety of spurious items were available. There were electronic items with names of famous brands inscribed on them; there were clothes with designer labels and many other items which could pass off as originals. They could be sold as original with discount offers in smaller cities and villages. But again, it would take time to buy the items, set up a shop, advertise them and then sell them. The logistics would take around one to two months – time that he didn't have.

But then he was a software engineer, an educated person who could build a solution out of a problem. He had been trained to solve tricky problems by building a logical path towards a desired solution. He could build software; all he needed was a wealthy client. But again, not only it would it take time, it would also be difficult to find a client within a short span of time. Also even if he was able to find a client, none will be able to give an advance of twenty lakhs for a job which will take a couple of months to get completed.

During his days as a student, he had also done a short course on ethical hacking ... could that help? Are there agencies that can pay him for ethical hacking? There are software companies who put their software to test by subjecting them to ethical hacking; there are banks, corporate, security agencies who hire hackers to break into their systems, in order to understand the vulnerabilities existing in their systems. But getting to them would involve another set of interviews, background checks and other procedures which will take another couple of months.

There were too many 'buts' in every solution coming to Abhi's mind. Each of the solution was viable, but not feasible to yield the desired result in the next eighteen days. He was hardly able to concentrate on his job and that had started showing on the regress of his current project. There has been no considerable progress on the part of the project he needed to complete in the next one month. The next day, he needed to put forward the status of his part in front of the department head, who in turn would judge the progress of the whole project.

Aditi, reaching her office early, switched on the server and all the systems, making the institute ready for the day.

The previous night had been quite restless with different ideas wandering through her mind. For one of her ideas, she now connected the internet on her system and opened a search engine to search for some important information. She surfed for an hour or so, noted down certain details in her diary and closed the tab. The official day had to be started. She went to the reception area and dialled certain phone numbers, which went unanswered. She looked at the watch; it was 8:45 a.m. Maybe it was too early for offices to open. She would try later. She went to the washroom, neatened herself and had a good look at herself in the mirror. She was pleased to look at her flawless face, a well-carved nose, artistic lips and dark black hair flowing down her shoulders, giving a contrasting background to her sharp featured face. She looked down at her neatly carved body and a smile floated on her oval red-coloured lips. Tying her hair, she came out and greeted the receptionist, who had just arrived, and went to her desk.

Abhi had been thinking all through the day. Time passed by and it was another evening with no solution. His head had begun to ache when Shashank came to his seat and started the conversation.

"It was a hectic day today. I had to rebuild the whole logic again to let the programme give relevant output," said Shashank.

"Oh, then it must have slowed down the whole cycle. What will you state in tomorrow's briefing?" enquired Abhi.

"But what about your part? I have been watching … you have also not been doing much today."

"Not much yaar, I am also behind schedule," said Abhi. "And now I am also getting a headache. I doubt I'll be able to stay late."

"Oh forget it, apart from you and me, Rajendra and Bhushan are also behind schedule, just be ready with an explanation and we all will be saved. You know, when four of the important team members are behind schedule, we are bound to get an extension apart from the chiding," consoled Shashank. "Now shut down your system and let's go have some beer, it's much needed now."

"Yes, I think that's a better idea. Just give me a minute."

"Sure, I will wait for you at the cigarette shop," said Shashank and went away.

Downstairs, Shashank lit a cigarette and crossed the road standing on the opposite side of the gate of the office. Pulling out his cell phone, he dialled a number from its phonebook. "Ah, yes Raghubhai, how are you? ... Yes we are going to a bar right now. I will check up with him and ... yes ... yes ... I will suggest it to him ... no, no just casually, I will only put the idea ... sure ... well Abhi is coming ... I will keep you posted, bye."

Shashank disconnected the call and waved to Abhi. Together they walked to the bar which was two blocks away.

They ordered beer for themselves.

"Well, these are tough days. Work pressure is increasing day by day," said Shashank.

"True! Gone are the days when my father used to work for eight hours including a lunch hour and that also at their own leisure," remarked Abhi.

The waiter brought the large beer mugs and two bottles of strong beer.

"In those days the requirements were less, life demanded less," continued Shashank. "Nowadays, due to the global phenomenon there are thousands of new items on the list and with better advertisement channels, their information reaches us even before the product is launched."

"Yes, it is a predetermined plan to create the demand for an item, launch it in the market and then make it a necessity," added Abhi.

"Of course, once the necessity of an item is created, then you are also made capable enough to buy it. You get finances in terms of loans, credit cards and all sorts of discounts and free gifts to lure you into buying it."

"This has become a vicious circle. What sages have long ago identified as a 'mayajal'; the more you let yourself get tempted, the more you get entangled into this spider web."

The waiter came again and placed a plate of peanuts.

Abhi and Shashank took their sips of beer and munched some peanuts.

"We ourselves have also got enmeshed into this web and now our lives are getting tossed in a frying pan," continued Abhi.

"But one notable thing is that the more we spend, we do devise ways to earn more as well. This has also led to different types of new professions around the globe. This has helped reduce unemployment and give rise to entrepreneurship," said Shashank.

"Yes, in a way, but ways of earning are limited and this has also given rise to earning by rogue means," said Abhi, finishing his first mug and pouring the rest of the beer from the bottle into his mug.

"Ah, the rogue way of earning reminds me of something recent," said Shashank laughing, "Someone gave me an offer last month for a temporary assignment of hacking into someone's system and was ready to pay in me in lakhs."

"So what did you do?"

"Refused, of course. I don't want to get involved in such messy jobs," said Shashank and signalled at the waiter for a refill.

"Yeah, they are very risky, and usually involve hacking into some government sites and turns you into a traitor before you know it," said Abhi.

"No, no … it was not a government site; it was some business rivalry case. Had to get details of some business secrets from one corporate for another. Pranam Enterprises or something like that. I didn't get into much of the details. The offer came by just in an informal talk at a friend's party," said Shashank.

"Yeah, I think business secrets are also very prized possessions these days. When was this offer made to you?"

"It was last month. Hey wait, are you thinking of taking up the job? Don't think of it. There's a good amount of risk involved," said Shashank

"No buddy, I am not interested," Abhi said casually.

"But one thing is for sure. There must be a huge amount of money involved … some fifteen to twenty lakhs, I think," said Shashank and finished his glass in one single go.

Abhi stared at his glass in a pensive mood for some seconds, lifted his gaze towards Shashank, bringing his beer mug up and finished it with a light smile on his lips. Shashank called for the bill.

Stepping out of the bar, a cool breeze hit their faces, elevating the intoxication and taking them to a mentally lighter state. Stretching themselves, they moved across the street towards the cigarette shop to have a smoke together.

"It was quite relaxing, we need breaks more often," said Abhi.

"I was quite fed up with today's job, just running the same queries again and again and still not getting the result. This drink has helped me clear my brain. I'll do better tomorrow," said Shashank.

"Tomorrow will be a new day. I hope something better for myself too. Let's pray things go as per our expectations," added Abhi. "Well, I should leave now. It's late and I need to get some rest before I embark on a new day."

"Yeah, we should," said Shashank, extending his hands for a goodbye shake.

"Good night then and see you tomorrow," Abhi turned to get his bike from the parking area.

Shashank watched him go and then pulling out another cigarette, lit up and started walking towards the auto stand. As he watched Abhi pass by him on his bike, he took out his cell phone. He whispered, "Hello, Yes I have floated the idea ... yes I think he seemed interested ... fine, bye then." Talking briefly and softly, he continued his walk towards the auto stand. The job seemed to have been done efficiently.

Feeling the cool air on his face inside the helmet, Abhi's mind was thinking about Pranam Enterprises. He had heard the name before. Driving attentively with a conscious effort, he reached his flat, opened the door and went straight to his bedroom, avoiding the dining table. Freshening up, he sat on the bed with his laptop on his lap. He searched for Pranam Enterprises. He then remembered that it was one of the companies with whom his own company, Solution Informatics was competing for some contract about one year back. It was some job at one of the manufacturing concerns where his company had won the contract in its favour for automation of several processes. Pranam Enterprises had been one of the other bidders. He visited its home site, checked on its 'contact us' tab and then closed down.

This firm was itself into technology, then why would it like to hire someone from outside for a hacking job, he wondered. Maybe they wanted a freelancer who could not be associated with their company. Shashank didn't tell him who had contacted him on behalf of this company or what data was to be hacked. If the company was ready to pay up to twenty lakhs for a single job, then this must be some big sport. Thinking about all this, he switched off the laptop. He got into bed and switched off the bedside light.

Lying in the dark with his eyes open, the thought of twenty lakhs for a single job kept flashing through his mind. He was not new to breaking into security tabs and secured gateways. Should he go for it? It was the only way to get so much money in such a short time. He got up again and connected his laptop, opened a search window again and typed 'Pranam enterprises' in the search engine and clicked 'enter'.

Several lakhs of entries were found in some nanoseconds. The first article was the home site of the company, the next some cached page and after that a requirement for a freelance network and software specialist for some temporary job. This article had been posted just two hours back. That meant the company was again in need of some freelancer. There was hope that the remuneration would be close to what Shashank had mentioned.

3rd Day

"**D**ad, you don't worry … business is just going fine and I am taking care of it quite nicely. You just enjoy your retirement. The turnover has been growing, profits are increasing, our presence among top clients is increasing, what else! Today we are among the top players in this field, but be assured, soon we will be *the* top player and that too with a huge margin …. Oh, don't worry about my health. I am going great. I never miss my fitness routine … By the way, Dad, I have to rush for a meeting. Will meet you after dinner. See you."

Rajal disconnected the web chat and switched over to his mailbox which flashed an important mail.

It has been a long time since he took over as CMD of his father's company. Over the period he has got good clients, and had been able to expand his company's reach to multiple sectors, providing software solutions in different areas. Rajal has been quick to identify talent from the market and has gone to poach them from existing companies. He had also been getting work done through freelancers.

The competition had also been tough in his field and Rajal had to keep an eye on his team to make sure they wouldn't freelance for competing companies. He was a good paymaster and kept himself updated on the personal requirements of his staff. This helped him to estimate the needs of his employees and continuously kept correcting the pay packages. But all this has not been easy, as this also required him to make an extra effort to continuously keep getting business to increase the turnover and profits.

Rajal's business tactics had been useful and he was successful in securing big deals. But as it happens in the competitive world, some other ambitious CEO also started offering competitive packages and tried to penetrate into the market. Rajal has also been aware of some companies that had been trying to venture in his field and have been offering predatory prices for the deals. It had been becoming difficult for him to counter them because of the low profile activities of the companies which had been able to afford this type of work at such low costs.

After talking to his father and checking the mail, Rajal stretched back on his chair and suddenly thought back on the event two years ago where he had met Aditi and offered her something which Indian girls usually do not accept. But at that time, he had become so obsessed with her that he couldn't stop himself from making the offer.

"Oh God, if she would have accepted ..." thinking aloud, Rajal had a smile floating on his lips. He could still remember those perfect curves and longed to have a feel of them. He had several times imagined her on his bed and had aroused himself thinking of having sex with her. He was unmarried and had never thought of marrying and getting entangled in a lifelong relationship; he had always believed in one night stands. Rajal had always been clear about his relations with women and had never promised any exclusivity to any of them. Many such relations had been forged and then amicably severed to be re-established at some future point of mutual need.

Aditi had been one incident which he could not successfully manoeuvre, maybe he had tried too early. But Rajal has never been a person to cry over a broken glass; he moved ahead to get a new glass for himself.

It is not easy to forget things which we long for. What we easily get does satisfy us for a short time, but what is difficult to achieve develops a craving which when satisfied gives an orgasmic satisfaction. Business successes had never been very exciting for Rajal; they were more of a challenge which he knew would consume some of his grey matter and ultimately make him victorious. He never hesitated in taking a step back to make way for two steps ahead and this had helped him achieve greater successes in his deals.

His father had started a shop selling radios, which developed into a big showroom of electronic equipments over a period of time. During the later part, while Rajal was still in his second year of B.Tech.(Computers), he incorporated a company for software development. It was after Rajal took over that the company developed from a small software development company to a corporate delivering technological solution at industry levels. Rajal's studies and his friend circle, along with the wave of globalization sweeping the times, helped his company grow into a multi-solutions provider technological corporate. His clientele included power, steel, FMCG, services and most other sectors where any technological upgradation was warranted for.

Since he had developed the business with his own efforts, he had complete knowledge of each and every nut and bolt of his company. Whenever any problem arose, he was ready with a solution, just like a medic. He knew which of his employees were doing what, who was expertizing in which field and who had what level of ambition. He was also aware of how rivals were always trying to poach his employees and even trying to squeeze out his company secrets. He always had an eye on his employees who may use their hacking skills to infiltrate his own secured data and sell them to his rivals. He has himself done a lot of research and development work in his systems to make them hacker proof, but still, he had to be vigilant.

As people reached their homes after another day's work, in another part of the city, Abhi clicked on a link on his laptop. He could hear the beats of his heart against his ribcage and his breath falling short. The page opened; it was a short description of the job, just detailing the requirement of a freelance software specialist who specialises in ethical hacking. A phone number was given in the end, with no mention of remuneration. Only the word 'urgent' kept on blinking in the top line; the same word was flashing in his head too.

A strange job ad, thought Abhi. He saved the number in his mobile's phonebook as 'Ghost' and decided to make the call the next day.

At the same time, Aditi sat in her room, looking at the television screen, her mind elsewhere. Before leaving office, she had again tried those numbers which she had noted earlier in the day, and this time, some calls were answered. After few more calls, she finally got one which seemed to be 'the' number. But before dialling the number, she had to think hard and make a final decision. Calling the number would have to be the last thing after completely making up her mind to tread on this un-retractable path. Her mind was speaking aloud to her and too fast to let her understand anything.

Usually people are advised to decide between what the heart says and what the mind suggests, but actually both are what the mind says. It is only a disguise which masks our thoughts with an emotional mask and a logical mask. Our brain is smart enough to give different options to some other part of our brain and then requires that department to work on the decision part. Aditi's brain was working on the decision making part as the options had already been explored.

Aditi thought over the incidents of the last few days and then contemplated over the options available. There was nothing new in her mind and the same dilemma continued. She put one pillow over her head, clutching it with her arms, pressing the pillow against her head, trying to calm down the rush of thoughts in her brain. Sleep finally overarched her thoughts and put her brain to rest till morning.

4th Day

Abhi entered the office and went straight to his cubicle. He started his system and connected to the network. It was 9:30 a.m. and he started downloading his mails. He had planned to call the 'Ghost' at 10:00 a.m. Other members of the staff had also arrived by this time. At 9:45 a.m., the boss called a meeting of all the staff members.

In five minutes, everyone gathered in the conference hall.

"Good morning everyone, it's nice to see all of you gather so quickly. Hope we remain this energetic all through the day. We have been doing a very good job and have got accolades from our customers for that. Recently, our senior management has received good feedback from our customers, but have also got a feel from the market that some of our competitors are trying to put hands on our developments and may lure our customers. The concern of the senior management is genuine as in the past, some of our clients had started using cheaper solutions with same efficiency from other companies. We need to remain involved in our developments and also keep an eye on the available solutions in the market. Our senior management is already thinking of gathering this market information through some unconventional ways. Meanwhile, we need to be alert and see that we do not discuss our work in progress with anyone outside this office, not even informally to our family and friends. We do not want to leak any information in any way. We need to protect secrecy of our job and of our client's requirements. Hope we understand and are very clear. Just be aware, that's all for the day. Thanking you all for giving me a patient ear." The boss finished his speech and immediately left the room.

Abhi concluded two things. The message was just downloaded from the top to bottom and that some 'unconventional' means will be used to gather market information. Was it pointing towards corporate espionage, and if so, did that include use of freelance computer specialists, may be hackers? Could this 'Ghost' be picking the call inside his own office?

Returning to his chair, Abhi's head was swimming with thoughts. His options again seemed to be narrowing down, bringing him to square one. He had to make a choice of calling the 'Ghost' at his risk. If it was not his own company, then he may achieve his goal; but if it was this company advertising under a pseudo name, then he was finished. But wait a minute! Shashank was contacted and if it would have been his own company, then why would it contact Shashank who was its own employee. After thinking a bit more on it, he decided to call the Ghost and check the feasibility once. Moreover, he had no other option in hand, and time was running fast. He had to do something, and if this call failed, he'd have to think of some way to disappear from this world along with his sister, who was an innocent victim. Abhi decided to make the call first.

Abhi dialled the number. It was answered politely by a lady. On understanding the purpose of the call and identifying the caller, she gave him another number to call.

The call was picked after three rings.

"Hello, how may I help you?" A male voice spoke in an authoritative tone.

"Hi, this is Abhimanyu Prakash, I had called in reference to a job post on the net, regarding a freelance software specialist."

"Oh yes, we had advertised, so you are a software engineer …"

"Yes, working primarily on development of software solutions".

"And have you worked on hacking techniques? You know, testing security setups and all that?"

"Yes, I have been good at that."

"Well, mail me your CV. I will check and inform you accordingly."

"Can we meet … today or tomorrow?"

"Oh, you seem to be in a hurry. Let me analyse your credentials and check if you suit our requirements, then only it will be beneficial to meet or we might end up wasting each other's time."

"Don't worry, I will not waste your time. We can meet and you can personally check my abilities."

"Well … Okay! Me at Hotel Tavern, room 209 today evening at six."

"Fine, I will be there."

"Good day, see you then."

"Thanks and good day."

Abhi was happy to have been able to secure an appointment. He saved this new number on his mobile as 'Ghost senior'.

On the other side of the phone, Rajal had a smile on his lips; the hurry in the tone gives away the neediness. The need creates a strong motivation.

◆

After supervising the first batch of students, Aditi sat on her chair and started to make up her mind on calling the number. Aditi stood in a huff and went outside to the balcony, which used to remain closed. It was exceptionally used by some staff member for smoking or having some private conversations on their phones. Aditi dialled the number and waited for the ring. Her heart was beating fast, her stomach seemed to be harbouring a thousand butterflies and sweat dripped on her forehead. As it kept ringing, she was going to disconnect when she suddenly heard, "Yes, Rajal here …"

Aditi remained quiet for a few seconds.

"Hello again, it's Rajal, what can I do for you?"

"Ah … Hi, Rajal … How are you?"

"I'm fine, thank you. But who am I talking to …?"

"I don't know whether you remember me. Aditi … we met two years back at a conference in Delhi."

"Oh hi Aditi! How are you? It's has been a long time … where are you?"

"Well, I have been here in this city and am fine … just felt like talking to you"

"I'm glad you still remember me, tell me what else is going on."

"Nothing, life as usual, just thought of meeting you sometime …"

"Good! I am free after seven today … if that is fine."

"Yes, it's fine … where?"

"I have a meeting at Hotel Tavern today evening. There is a cafe nearby called Caffeno. Will see you there."

"I'll wait for you."

"Bye then and see you."

Aditi disconnected and let out a huge sigh.

The first chapter was over …

Rajal kept looking at the receiver in his hand for a few seconds and then placing it on the cradle, leaned back on the chair, stretched and smiled ... was it the hunting season?

Aditi finished her rounds of supervision and whatever teaching she had to do and packed up by 4:00 p.m. She excused herself, feigning slight illness to her colleagues. She had to reach home early to get ready for the evening. She had to look really gorgeous.

✦

By 5:00 p.m., Abhi was ready to leave office. Though it was a bit early, he needed some time to compose himself and be ready for a meeting where he had to break a deal. There was a cafe named Caffeno near the hotel where he could have a cup of coffee and relax for sometime before joining hands with his would be employer.

✦

Aditi reached home by 4:30 p.m. She opened her almirah and started glancing through her dresses. Choosing a dress for an occasion had never been easy for her. Especially for this occasion, where she had to meet a person whom she doesn't like at all, but had to seduce. She took out her green suit, put it on her in front of the mirror, and turned sideways to check the fit of the dress and its side flows. Smiling, she took it off and kept it on the bed, rushing towards her dressing table to decide the colour of lipstick, nail paint, blushes, perfumes and all the other necessities.

Abhi ordered a milk coffee with some nutty cookies and had both of them in total silence, looking at the people and vehicles going and coming. Life was going on as usual out there, but his life had turned upside down. How simple things sometimes threaten the very existence of something more important and precious such as life! Money is never so difficult to earn, but it is the time and manner in which it is earned that poses risks to life. Millions of lives are lost across the world just because of this petty issue which becomes so important at some point of time that nothing else remains in sight and human lives are lost in pursuit.

Aditi looked at her image in the mirror. Then she stood straight and stared appreciatively at her image.

"Gorgeous babe," she mumbled to herself. Aditi clutched her handbag and before leaving the room re-assured of her looks, and kissed her image goodbye.

Later in the hotel room, Abhi seated himself on the sofa and felt butterflies in his stomach. Rajal on the opposite sofa was going through Abhi's CV.

"Well then I am looking for a person who can break into systems and check the security protocols ... your CV is quite good. If I may say, It nearly fits to what our expectations, but you know we are not going to employ full time and need only freelance service for which you will be paid handsomely," said Rajal.

"I understand sir, I am already employed and have no intentions of leaving that job; just want to utilise my free time and earn some bucks on the go ..."

"Well, so we have an understanding. But any legal issues due to your employment contract with your present employer will have to be handled by you and we will not be a party to that ... the same will be incorporated in our contract and legally we will presume you are presently not employed with anyone else as per our knowledge, and that requires you to submit a fresh CV which does not have any reference to your present employment status."

"That would be fine with me. I will give you a fresh CV and assure you of no such issues cropping up from my employer's side in future."

"Okay, so we will discuss the job once you submit your fresh CV and we will formally sign a contract of employment. That will take approximately two weeks and then we will start".

"Two weeks!" exclaimed Abhi in dismay.

"Yes, it will take this much time at least ... hope you are fine with that."

"Oh yes, but can it be given some extra momentum and other processes speeded up as I would like to finish the job in the next two weeks itself ..."

"Finish the job in next two weeks? Are you kidding! It is the job of testing and will take more time. You will have to sit with my programmers and help them design stronger security measures ... it will take time, my friend ..."

Abhi, frowning at the delay and expecting the worst to come, said, "And what will be the remuneration for the job, if I may ask?"

"Oh yes, we will be paying a lump sum of fifty thousand bucks per assignment after deducting taxes," Rajal took out a cigarette from the pack and tucked it between his lips.

"Fifty thousand per assignment? Well, I was expecting something more ... actually I *needed* something more. And I also expected a higher level of difficulty which would justify my requirement."

"Well Mr Abhimanyu, I think we have a disconnect somewhere. My company is looking at getting a testing professional who is an expert in breaking soft barriers and use the expertise to develop some other tools. We don't think we satisfy your expectations. I think you have some other target in your mind. It was nice talking to you ... hope we do business together sometime, thank you."

Rajal stood up and extended his right hand; a sign for Abhi to get up and get going.

"Thank you sir," Abhi got up, shook hands lightly and turned towards the door. Rajal sat down on the couch.

Shashank had referred to a larger amount closer to his requirement, but was this that same job? Or had he mistakenly selected the wrong advertisement. The last few days started coming in like a thumb strip in front of his eyes as his hands reached the door knob.

"By the way, what is your requirement ... just wanted to know." Rajal's voice was heard along with the smell of burning tobacco.

"Well, no use really, as it's too high and urgent too ..." replied Abhi casually with his hand opening the door slightly.

"Sometimes opportunities come in disguise ... we should never lose hope."

Abhi let his grip loose on the knob and turned towards Rajal, "I actually needed twenty lakhs and that too by this fortnight ... let's see how it materialises."

"Gosh! Twenty lakhs in the next fifteen days! Are you kidding?"

"Need to resolve some urgent issue."

"It's a lot more money to be earned in just fifteen days. Any plans on how you will go about it?" quizzed Rajal.

"Not yet. I was of the view you might have some big job to offer, which can maybe pay me handsomely closer to my requirement. I think I was living in a dream world to think of getting this amount from some job. It was foolish of me," answered Abhi

"I don't know if I should ask, but what is the urgent need for this amount?"

"Well, that is personal, can't discuss, but yes, it's not anything illegal ..."

"But earning that much in so little time may involve some illegality," probed Rajal further.

"Presently, the need is too important to think of the ways of earning. I just need to have this amount at any cost," a frustrated Abhi grinned and turned back again to open the door. That's when he heard, "I can give it to you, but ..."

"But!?" Abhi turned closing the door behind him, a spark igniting in his eyes.

"I am not sure whether you would like to do the job. Actually, there is something which came across my mind vaguely while looking at your CV. I can think of expending that much money if I get the desired result, and time is no problem for the same," Rajal said, slowly emphasising on each word coming out of his mouth.

Abhi kept staring at Rajal for a few moments. Rajal looked up at him, and reading his eyes, asked, "Would you like to take a seat and see if we can be of use to each other?"

Abhi closed the door firmly and walked towards the sofa. Sitting on the edge of the sofa clinching his file with both hands, he looked towards Rajal attentively. "Yes, I am listening. Is it something illegal?"

"No, no, not exactly illegal," laughed Rajal. "Well, when we call it ethical hacking, it means we are presuming there will be unethical hacking and to ensure it does not happen, we promote it as a testing to secure ourselves from an unethical one. But what if a little unethical can earn you twenty lakhs ... is it worth it?"

"Is it a government site??" questioned Abhi, becoming curious as he had already come mentally prepared for this.

"No, we are businessmen, not terrorists or spies. We first see profits and business opportunities and do not get involved with the government. We just want to earn some more and can invest enough to maximise profits," explained Rajal.

"How many days' project is this?"

"It depends on your capability."

"How much money can be paid?"

"I told you ... your need can be fulfilled."

"Twenty lakhs?" Abhi said sheepishly.

"Hmm ..."

"If I complete the job in fifteen days, when will I be paid?"

"Within an hour of completion of the job," said Rajal, "but of course, to my satisfaction."

Abhi was looking at the carpet, thinking hard. He looked up and then with excitement spoke out, "What is the job?"

✦

It was around 7:10 p.m. when Rajal, sitting at one of the corner tables in Caffeno, looked towards the cafe entrance through which a gorgeous lady entered. Her long shiny hair covering half of her right eye along with a portion of the cheek fell over the shoulder. The v-shaped neckline of her green suit ended just where it all started. Her white polished hands clutched a small purse while her eyes wandered around the cafe. Then she saw him and smiled a little. So she was really Aditi.

"Gorgeous," mumbled Rajal while getting up to welcome her with a smile.

Aditi came swinging around a bigger table in the centre and stretched her hands towards Rajal. Rajal took her hand gladly, greeting her quite warmly, having none of the past bitterness. Both casually avoided any mention of their last encounter.

"So, you look the same after all these years; still the same young Rajal," admired Aditi while taking her chair.

"But you seem to have grown younger and more gorgeous. I just couldn't recognise you … How is your job?" Rajal quickly changed the topic.

"Just fine, teaching is itself a new learning every day."

"Yeah, I understand. By the way, what will you have with your old espresso?"

"Just a patty, that's all."

Rajal signalled to the waiter and placed the order.

"You have grown up to be a big businessman. You have a good presence in the market," said Aditi.

"Yes, I have expanded my father's business and have also ventured into new areas, lots of projects in hand."

"So you were in the neighbourhood for some business deal, I suppose?"

"Hmm … a business proposition. Let's see, trying to go in for something bigger," replied Rajal.

The waiter brought two coffees and two patties. Aditi meanwhile was wondering how to go forward.

"It must be tough out there, managing the business and handling all this competition," Aditi said.

"It is difficult, but then it has its own benefits. You can make your work life adapt itself to you."

"Yeah, no choice I guess," sighed Aditi.

"Challenges are one thing and comfort is another. In your own business, you have to continuously be on your toes and keep searching for new assignments. In a job, you only need to do what you are assigned to, not having to give much thought on where the next day's job comes from," said Rajal.

"Hmm … I have to agree, even though the other side seems to be more comfortable and this illusion keeps our lives going and growing," said Aditi.

"Don't you think we are wandering towards philosophy now? Come on! It's life and we are here to have coffee for old times' sake. By the way how, after so many years, did you think of me? I never thought you'd want to remember me after …"

"Life moves on … it's better not to look back," interrupted Aditi.

For some seconds there was silence, both looking deep into their coffee mugs.

"So how is your wife?" Aditi started again.

"Wife! How could you think I am married?" exclaimed Rajal.

"Well, a successful man like you cannot be a bachelor for too long. Success brings with it the responsibility of sharing and raising a family of one's own," explained Aditi.

Rajal laughed slowly and said, "I am still in search of success, and then, by the logic you gave, I am still not ready to bear this responsibility."

"Success is always a never-ending search. You have to decide when it is enough to satisfy your needs. Anything more is just an infinite search," said Aditi.

"Do you want some more coffee?" asked Rajal.

Aditi looked at her cup; it was empty, and so was Rajal's. It signalled the end of their meeting session but she was still nowhere close to saying what she had come to say. She had to find a way to tell him her real intention.

"No, thanks but you can order one for yourself. I am in no hurry," replied Aditi trying to buy some more time.

"Yes, I will have one more as I don't get much free time to have coffee," said Rajal and waved to the waiter.

"So you are still teaching or have you switched your profession?"

"No, I am still there, where else can I go?" replied Aditi, trying to judge each word spoken, trying to manipulate how to mould the conversation to the right direction.

"Why don't you think of taking up a job in some industry where you can apply your knowledge to create better solutions?" suggested Rajal.

"A job is after all just another job. I sometimes think of doing something of my own. You know, some entrepreneurial stuff, something where I create what I want to create," said Aditi, with an idea bulb shining over her head. This conversation now could help in her motive.

"So you want to start your enterprise, it's a good thought."

"But it's just a thought. I am still dependent on my salary and thinking of being an entrepreneur is something easier said than done."

"Why, if you have a thought and a will to do something, you can always achieve it. That's a proven fact," said Rajal sipping his hot coffee.

"You can say that since you got a running business to expand further, Mr Rajal; to *start* a business, there is a need to have a fund and usually a gestation period to start any earning."

"Yes, I understand, but where there is a will, there is a way. It's an old saying but true in every age. Believe me, you will get what you want once you start believing that you really want it," said Rajal.

"The way I plan to start will require nearly twenty lakhs and it's a lot of money to save from my salary. By the time I will reach this figure, the requirement will become at least ten times of it," replied Aditi slyly.

Rajal was amused hearing the same amount for the second time that day. "Why don't you check out with some bank or financial institution?"

"They will need some documents of past experience in business, and most importantly, the money needs to be returned while I am not sure whether I will be able to even retain the investment, let alone earning over it … so it has to be money which I can afford to lose without having to stress myself on the returning part. And you know that can happen only with one's own money and not borrowed money," explained Aditi.

"Okay, so you plan to start your business when you are about to leave this world," laughed Rajal.

"Maybe … or maybe I need to wait for some miracle to happen and some old relative of mine to die leaving a fortune for me," Aditi added to the laughter.

Rajal again burst into laughter and while he was laughing he heard, "Or maybe someone has an offer for me, the same one which you offered two years ago …"

Rajal looked at Aditi, she was smiling a bit, blushing more.

Rajal lifted his cup, finished the coffee in one go and called the waiter for the bill. Aditi didn't say anything, just kept looking at other tables, while Rajal stared at the empty cup. Finally Rajal put some cash on the table and stood up saying, "Let's go now."

"Yes, let's go. It was nice chatting with you, will catch up sometime," said Aditi getting up.

They both came out of the cafe. On the doorstep Rajal said, "Shall I drop you somewhere?"

"No thanks, I will walk a little from here. Have a friend nearby, will visit her," said Aditi.

"Okay then bye, see you again sometime." Rajal shook hands with Aditi and then turned to cross the street.

Aditi saw him walking away towards a hotel. She turned right and after walking some ten steps, called a cab and sat in it. Sitting in the cab her heart beating fast, she let it sink in that the step has been taken. Life may change.

She threw her head back and closed her eyes. The move had been made.

5th Day

It's a new morning with new hope. Abhi got up fresh and got ready for office much quicker than usual. Then he went into the kitchen to help Aditi make breakfast. Omelettes and juice or coffee was their regular. Abhi had his breakfast hurriedly and left as soon as possible, without looking at Aditi.

Poor Abhi, he looks too terrified to meet my eyes now, thought Aditi while holding her glass of juice. But don't worry bro, your sister will arrange something; after all, it's me who is at stake now.

Abhi entered his office slowly as if entering someone's house with an intention of stealing. His conscience was pinching him of having agreed to work for someone else. This was equivalent to treachery and his conscience was pricking him for this wrongdoing. He went to his desk and looked around sheepishly as if to check if anyone had caught him talking to a rival company. Abhi opened his system and started working on the already delayed project. But it was becoming difficult for him to concentrate. He was still not sure what job he was required to do, but guessed it must be something which he would have refused had he not been in this fix. Mr Rajal had promised to meet him again that evening to fill him in about the requirements and the exact timeline by which he was required to complete the job, though he was given a preliminary that it would relate to obtaining a rival business secret and not anything anti-national.

Abhi had been thinking a lot about the job he may be required to do. He may have to hack into some site and steal some data, for marketing purpose or maybe to steal some software or break the code of some e-locker to get useful information. It would be better if it did not require breaking into some government secrets or some bank accounts, but even if it is so, was he in a position to refuse? With hardly fifteen days left, he had to first get the money and then think of its consequences. He just could not think of letting Aditi face any music for his actions. He had to do everything to prevent what he had been threatened of. Talking to Raghubhai again crossed his mind, but he brushed aside the idea as those men cannot be talked to; they prefer becoming physical with the slightest of provocation.

It was the fifth day and though things seemed to be going his way, not even a single event could assure him of the desired results. All doors seemed closed and the way to a solution seemed too long. What should be done, he thought; hope, expectation, gloom, fear ... everything at the same time was draining his life energy out.

"Hey Abhi, are you coming, just going for a smoke," shouted Shashank from the fire exit door. Abhi waved in affirmation and locked his system screen before getting up.

"So what were you so engrossed in? Stuck somewhere?" queried Shashank.

"No, just trying to concentrate more; we are already behind schedule and need to bridge the time gap."

"Really, I thought you would complete it today and then we'd all get a nice beating, 'Look Abhi has finished and you all are just sitting on it' and blah, blah, blah," ridiculed Shashank

"Oh come on, give me a break. No talk about work during smoking, and yes, I will also have some puffs today."

"Okay, so there is some real brain burning going," laughed Shashank.

Abhi appreciated the simile; his brain was really burning out and he needed some time off to cool it down. Shashank lit up the cigarette and after inhaling it twice, handed it to Abhi. Abhi took one long drag and held his breath for a few seconds before releasing the excess smoke. Closing his eyes, he could feel the spin in his head. He took another deep puff before passing the butt back.

"Well, I think we will get further delayed ... unless each of us individually completes our part, the merging could not start and the crafting of final shape will get initiated only after that," said Shashank between puffs.

"Yes and soon we are going to have a review meeting also, which I suppose will be more painful than stretching some extra hours to complete it."

"Indeed, it will be, so let's get back and bury ourselves in our screens and enjoy," laughed Shashank, throwing the butt as he waved at Abhi to follow him back to the work floor.

✦

She had made a move the previous evening, but now Aditi's brain was also smoking up, planning the next step. Time was short and moves were many. She had no choice; the end result had to be achieved. She could not wait for a response from him for long and needed to meet him again, but how? What should be the occasion? In order to divert her mind away so that some fresh thoughts could make inroads into her, she opened her Facebook page and started checking out what her other friends were up to. Megha was back from Manali, and had posted photos of herself holding snowballs in both her hands, Anuj had shared some post on a needy man, Rekha had changed her profile picture and was looking more dreadful. There were many new friend requests, which Aditi ignored unless it was someone close. There were some friend suggestions which she browsed through, finding no one of much interest. She again went to the home page, but there were no new stories. Getting bored, she logged off to get some coffee. Aditi pulled out one coffee from the vending machine and as she threw herself on the chair, something clicked in her head.

Aditi logged in to her Facebook account again, went to the find friends section and entered Rajal in the search field. The photograph attached with the first Rajal itself matched with the one she was looking for. She immediately sent a friend request and then went back to her own profile. She searched for her photos stored on the PC and changed her profile picture to a more tempting one. Taking a sigh of relief, she logged out and relaxed, sipping her coffee.

◆

After attending a conference call with all his senior engineers, Rajal was quite satisfied that he would be able to bag the project and its successful completion would add one more star to his company's ever improving profile and brand image. But still, he could leave nothing to chance and as always, the strings have to be in his control to let the play run as per his command. Earlier too, though he had been able to grab projects based on his own merit, there had been some which he had lost and these were his sour wounds which he needed to heal. This time, the project was big and would have an industry-wide impact. This project would make him the most renowned service provider in this field and would also provide him a monopolistic edge. This edge, if carried on for even the next five years, would bring his company into the top league.

Rajal swivelled his chair towards the window, looking out from his eleventh floor office at the traffic running below. The atmosphere seemed nice outside, but then Rajal realised his windows were covered with black UV films and his cabin was cooled by a good two-ton air conditioner to a temperature of twenty degrees. He smiled at how one's own condition changes the outlook for others. Rajal was toying with his smartphone and he opened the Facebook application. His eyes first went to the friend request bar which had been prominently showing the figure of eight. Opening the tab, he could instantly see the request by Aditi which he heartily accepted, another six he rejected and one he kept in abeyance. Then he checked Aditi's changed profile picture and smiled; it was much better than her earlier one.

Rajal kept looking at Aditi's new profile photo and started analysing the fact that the profile picture had been changed just when the friend request was placed. The earlier photo had a simple straight face with a tied braid in a simple yellow suit. But this one was totally different; she was exposing her bare back in a long backless red ensemble with her face turning back from left and her black shiny hair freely flowing on her right. The lips were half open with a dark red lip gloss matching her dress and her right hand raised up with palm down in a gesture of giving away her hand. The eyelids were slightly down with a drunken expression, as if she was submitting herself to be taken. Rajal, lost in appreciating the beauty of the photograph, suddenly felt his other hand rising, as if to go and caress her cheeks and hold her hand. He felt an erection. With a smile, he suddenly put down his phone and moved his eyes towards the window. Looking outside, he relaxed his thoughts and the other organs of his body. "Relax, the time will come and very soon it seems," Rajal mumbled to himself.

6th Day

Being a Sunday, Abhi was still in bed when his mobile rang. When he saw that Ghost Senior was calling, he immediately got up and took the call. After the usual pleasantries, it was understood that he had to meet Rajal in half an hour at an open air food joint two kilometres from his apartment building. He immediately got up and rushed to freshen up. In ten minutes he was waving for an auto rickshaw. It took around six minutes to reach the place and after paying the auto, Abhi stood under a tree on the side lane adjoining the joint. It was an open counter, self servicing food joint where you could order on the right side and get your order delivered on the left side of the counter. You could use the high tables to eat standing, or sit inside your own car. Abhi wondered why he had been called there, of all places. He saw Rajal coming towards him, dressed formally in a business suit and a tie.

"Come on, let's have some coffee," Rajal said as he ordered two cups of coffee. They then walked towards a large car parked nearby with their coffees. Rajal sat on the driver seat and Abhi beside him on the passenger seat.

"So, you wanted to know what the job was during our last meeting. I had asked you to first make up your mind that whatever is the job, it is the money you want and you will not let your conscience come in between. So, have you made up your mind?" asked Rajal sipping his coffee.

"Of course, otherwise I wouldn't have come," replied Abhi.

"Even if I say it involves your own company?" said Rajal.

Abhi sipped his coffee, looked outside the front glass, remembered Raghubhai, Aditi and the remaining fourteen days, "Yes, I am ready to do it, but I want all the money on the day I finish my job."

"That's my promise, within an hour of the job completion," assured Rajal.

"So what is it that you want me to do? Plant a bug?" asked Abhi.

"Something like that. You have your MD sitting a floor above you. I want access to all his communications."

"But that can be done through phone tapping and you can get it done at ten percent of the money you're offering me by bribing a telecom guy, why me?" said Abhi.

"Your MD doesn't communicate official details on the phone; he uses a laptop for his official documents which he rarely connects to the company's official net. He uses the desktop in his office for all non-secret official communications. But he never sends important communication through mail from his office desktop to his clients as it is prone to be intercepted. He uses his laptop and connects it to his home network or through any other private connection when he is required to send any classified documents or communication to his clients or confidants. I need the communication which is sent from his laptop," explained Rajal. "He keeps his laptop with himself all the time and works offline on it while he is in office."

"That would need hacking into his mailbox installed on his laptop or the whole data stored in the laptop to get the complete information which will take longer than I have," said Abhi.

"Well, time is not my problem, it's yours," smiled Rajal.

For next few minutes, both kept quiet. Abhi opened the door and stepped out. "Yes, it is my problem and I will solve it. Keep the amount ready; I need it as early as possible," he said while shutting the car door behind him.

Rajal took the last sip, lowered the window pane an inch and threw the cup out. He put the car into reverse and turned towards the main road; that day's job was over.

7ᵗʰ Day

Abhi had a long day picking bugs in his part of the software and putting it down on a chart paper to find the solution later. He brought the chart paper home and hung it on his room's wall to enable him to focus on the bugs. But sitting on his bed, his mind wandered to the other job Rajal had given him. It was the most important thing for him at this point of time. With just a few more days, he had to prioritise his thinking for that job.

'Well, time is not my problem, it's yours.' Rajal's words kept reverberating in his mind and he was not able to think about his next step. There was a risk about every part of the job given to him. Information was to be extracted and then passed on to Rajal. There should not be loss of any vital details and it had to be ensured every time such information was created and procured. Each risk point had to be covered and goal achieved without getting caught.

Abhi took another chart paper and started making points, drawing pictorial presentation of all activities to be done, connecting them serially to make a chronological flowchart. Then he started picking out the flows having maximum risks and those having minimum risks. The maximum risks were in two points: entering the system every time to extract information and then delivering it to the destination. If caught at any of these points, the whole activity would be rendered useless. Hence these two points had to be secure in a way that left no trail leading to the person initiating the processes. It should be a one-time activity, eliminating the requirement of a hacker's interaction with the system every time. This meant Abhi would have to think of a process where a one-time risk was taken to establish a one-sided pipeline from the MD's system to Rajal, so that information flows automatically without any hindrance or intervention. Introducing malware by hacking LAN or accessing a system by any other means was futile, since high security software were already installed in all their company's systems, and specially on his targeted system.

Time was running out and the brainstorming was being done with all available options, from breaking the mail ID password to getting malicious software inserted which could create a mirror system on some other remote hardware. But all these options were neither risk free nor detection proof. Also, in order to insert any malware, he would have to personally visit the system and upload the same from an external device. Mr Uday Singh, MD, Solutions Informatics, his company's boss always mailed important emails using his own personal data connection instead of using the company's network. All his important documents were stored in one of the external hard disks attached through USB port which denied any scanning request from the company's domain. It was not possible to scan any data on this hard disk until authorised by Mr Uday Singh himself with his finger print password.

After full three hours of brainstorming and exploring all options, Abhi gave up, as his head had started to roll over and his pineal gland was hot enough, ready to blast. He went to the washroom to release some of his liquid intake taken sip by sip.

He washed his face and forehead to cool down the overworked engine in his head. A little refreshed, Abhi gulped down a glass of chilled water to divert his attention from an aching brain to the bruised throat. A new pain created to kill another pain. Having diverted his brain, he tried to avoid looking at the chart paper, but then another part of his brain reminded him of Raghubhai and the approaching deadline.

In the adjoining room, Aditi was also engrossed in deep thought, trying to figure out her next move. Would Rajal take the bait or was he a reformed man? How should she take the proposal forward in a way that would save her from embarrassment? She remembered how she had refused Rajal's proposal years ago, so why was she expecting Rajal to accept hers now? For the last few days, she had been acting like a teenage girl trying to impress someone with her feminine traits. Rajal didn't seem to be that bad. He had never forced himself on her. Rajal had never even tried to use his financial strength to approach her in any other indecent way.

Suddenly Aditi realised she had started to accept Rajal in an affirmative way. Rajal, who had been the primary reason of her maintaining a distance from other male species, had unexpectedly changed. Had she started liking him or was it just a temporary phase? It was just that since she had to get her job done, her mind was trying to condition her in a way where she was able to accept her closeness with Rajal. Or was it that she had always liked him in some way, but had been successfully suppressing it? Is it that though the proposal seemed indecent,she had herself been expecting it in a more decent or cultured way or maybe it was her own guilt of societal customs? Who knows if Rajal had not been so straightforward and blunt earlier, she might have accepted the proposal. Was she repenting? Whatever it was, she remembered him as she was in a fix, expecting him to be the same Rajal. She had to go for it; there was no option but to succeed. Her own inhibitions and feminine guilt had no place as she had to take the step. Aditi shrugged and with a smile got up to switch off the lights. As her room plunged into darkness, she could see rays of light peeping from under the door, coming from the adjoining room. Maybe Abhi was also engaged in some part time job to arrange the required amount. But such a huge amount surely wouldn't be easy. That's where Aditi would pitch in.

"Good night," murmured Aditi, seeing off yet another day with not much progress.

8th Day

A bhi got up wondering whether he had slept or had been awake all night after the brainstorming marathon. He glanced at the chart paper hung on the wall and lazily went to the washroom. Half an hour later, he was still not feeling fresh. He went to pick the newspaper at the door, after which he went to the balcony with a glass of lemon water to read the newspaper, expecting like everyday to read the news which will proclaim that Raghubir and all his goons had died in some accident. On the sixth page, one headline caught his eye. He read the whole article about how a research agency had found new ways of introducing malwares in the PCs and smart phones with the help of USB attached devices. It said that systems and antivirus softwares were usually equipped to detect malwares through software written on its memory, but were not able to scan the firmware that controls the functioning of devices connected through the USB. And through these, hackers could induct malwares using small low cost chips which could control functioning of these USB devices.

This was interesting. It opened an opportunity and Abhi's brain started joining some more points based on the fresh piece of information it had just received.

With renewed vigour, Abhi jumped on his feet to go analyse the chart again, put some more points and change the course of a few other points. The day was short and much was required to be done, so he started to get ready for office. In the other room, Aditi was still sleeping and dreaming of some exotic experiences which had been crossing her mind for the last few days.

✦

Rajal had to get ready early that morning as he had to attend the award ceremony in the afternoon. The function was to start at 3:00 p.m. but the function was at a resort hotel in the neighbouring scenic hilly city about two hundred kilometres away. It would take around six hours to drive there. He had planned to reach the highway leading out of the city by nine so that he was able to reach the venue by half past two. By eight, Rajal was holding the steering of his car and was out of his house. He had to pick Alka, his General Manager Projects who was going to go along with him. They had to return the same day as the function was expected to be over by six.

He had promised to pick Alka from her house by 8:30 a.m. Usually his driver drove him to office, but Rajal loved driving, so whenever he had to go on a long journey by road, he himself took to the steering. As he drove to Alka's house, his thoughts wondered to Aditi. She was one girl who had for the longest period become a part of his routine thought process. Maybe somewhere secretly he had fallen in love, but did not want to accept it. Drowned in his thoughts, he reached Alka's house and honked once. Alka came out of the front door through the lawn and coming on the driver's side, invited Rajal for a coffee. Rajal refused and asked Alka to hurry up. Alka again went in and brought her bag, taking the passenger side, waving goodbye to her husband. Rajal moved the gear shaft to the first and drove towards the street leading out to the highway.

Though there was not much traffic on the streets, it took another half an hour for Rajal to arrive on the highway leading out of the city. Rajal and Alka had a normal employer-employee relationship. They started talking about their new project and were discussing further modalities when Rajal had to suddenly apply the brakes, as some bovine animals were crossing the road. They had to wait for some minutes for the cows to clear the way. He again pushed the lever to the first gear as he felt the back of his hand brushing the denim on Alka's thigh. It gave Rajal a momentary zing and then as his car caught some speed, he pulled the lever back to second gear, again brushing her thigh. This time again it was unexpected, as he had expected Alka to pull in her thigh after the first brush, but it seemed the thigh was protruding even more towards the gear knob. Pushing to third and then fourth gear, Rajal remembered her coming out of her house with her soft curly hair in a loose pony tail and a pink T shirt over a tight blue denim jeans. She was a beautiful lady, happily married, and a mother of a five-year-old boy. She still seemed like a bubbly teenager. Rajal suddenly began to have naughty thoughts about the stunningly beautiful girl sitting beside him. Should he be getting some signals?

In a bid to test his instincts, his eyes started looking for a tea stall. In another ten minutes, he found a tea stall by the side of the highway. He slowed down and parked in front of the shop. "Let's have some tea," said Rajal while pulling over.

"But you just refused my coffee as it was getting late," Alka said sarcastically.

"Oh come on! A roadside tea break is different," smiled Rajal.

"Okay," said Alka coming out of the car.

The street side cheap cup of tea in an earthen pot smells nicer and tastes better than the ten times costly cup of tea in large multi-star hotels. Rajal was in a hurry to finish the cup and restart his journey. He was too eager to put the car in first gear.

Finishing their tea and paying off, they got back into the car. The lever moved to the first gear and there it was, the much awaited and expected brush of the backhand with the denim. Rajal had by now thought out how to handle it. He turned his head and looked towards the lever in his hand, smiled and glanced up towards Alka, who was looking out of the front screen, but slowly turned towards Rajal. And yes, she was smiling too. Both kept the gaze locked with each other for about ten seconds and then Alka turned her face away, blushing and shying, caressing the strands of hair falling on her cheek, still smiling. Rajal released the clutch, moving the car ahead slowly and then pulling the lever back to second gear, this time pressing harder into Alka's thigh. As the car sped ahead, he changed gears successively to third and fourth, freeing his hand from the lever and slowly resting his palm on Alka's thigh. Alka didn't budge and sensing no adverse reaction, Rajal tightened his clutch on her thigh. Alka felt the pain and put her hand on Rajal's. Rajal placed his hand on hers. Alka turned towards Rajal, while he kept looking at the road ahead. He kept driving silently, feeling equal pressure inside and giving a serious thought on his next move.

Driving silently holding Alka's hand, he noticed an abandoned building structure which could once have been an old dhaba. He slowed down the car and took it towards the deserted structure. There was no one around; he took the car around the building and turned towards the back of the building behind a large wall. On the other side was a vast agricultural land. His car was now totally hidden from the main highway. Rajal stopped the car but kept the engine running to keep the air-conditioning functioning. He then turned towards an astonished Alka and pulled her towards him. Alka smiled back.

Rajal pulled himself closer to Alka and released his left hand taking it to Alka's face pushing her strands of hair behind her ear, caressing her cheek with his palm, and then sliding the palm through her ears towards her back. He clutched her hair and pulled her face towards his own. Alka let herself be overtaken by Rajal and slowly passed her hands through Rajal's sides, clutching the back of his hair tightly, pulling him completely inside her with her lips trying to squeeze out all the juices from Rajal's lips. For a minute or two, both remained engaged in a fulfilling and completely luscious kiss trying to overpower each other.

Their lips had already given way to their tongues and both kept enjoying each other's eternally orgasmic taste with eyes closed, absolutely oblivious to the space and time around. Having exhausted their breath with the luscious French kiss, Rajal began kissing Alka's cheeks, chin, ear, neck and was going lower when Alka took over and began kissing Rajal's neck, opening his shirt's top three buttons. Rajal while enjoying Alka's kisses on his bare chest. He took out her hair clip, freeing her hair from its clutches and sunk his face into her shiny black hair.

Engrossed in each other they made time stand still taking in each other's odour and submerging themselves in each other's bodies. Having satiated their thirst, they slowly released their grip and then superficially locked their lips again, not wanting to give up on each other. Engaging for some time, they slowly separated. Rajal kissing Alka on her palm and slowly slipping out his hand. Alka took out a comb from her handbag to comb her hair. Looking into the sun visor mirror, she applied her lip gloss again and turned at Rajal who was still watching her. Rajal smiled and once again caressing her cheeks turned the key in the ignition. Coming out on the highway, the car took to speed in no time as now with enhanced vigour there was a hurry to reach the destination to complete the act left in abeyance.

✦

Reaching office, Abhi had no interest in the ongoing project which was nearing its deadline, but logged on to the net to find as much material on external devices attached to the computer systems and their related technologies. There was a lot to understand, but the available time did not allow him to go into in-depth study. For the next three hours or so, he studied the basic technology behind these external devices, specially the chip architecture and related interaction between these devices. The response of a device or the system responses towards these devices were his special interests for now. Whenever a hard external device is connected to a computer, the detection process involves identifying the device, and the driver software within the device which then generates an acceptability response within the processing chambers of the computer. This response was the key to his plans. He did not have time to access the worldwide research which had already gone into malware induction through external devices, but had to design a low cost device with a malware inducting capability to acquire desired results in the given time. The first thing was to decide on the end result required. The previous night's brainstorming had taught him that since repeated entry into the system was a high risk area, he had to limit himself to a single entry task and then let the beneficiary himself take the risk of multiple entries.

The method decided would be to introduce a one-time malware which would do a permanent invisible change to the basic operating system, making every activity done on the system to be transmitted to a remote console. Having sat continuously for the last four hours and at least six coffees later, he started feeling the need to release some toxic liquid from his body. Shutting down the monitor, he raced towards the washroom. While washing his hands he felt the need to splash his face with some cold water to freshen up his brain. Abhi started staring at his own eyes in the mirror, trying to guess what was going on in the mind of the face in the mirror. Having stood still and staring at himself, suddenly his mind clicked on the word 'mirror image'. Yes! The mirror image. That was it! He needed to transmit a mirror image of the primary system to the remote console. This would require only a one-time entry into the system and then there would only be transmission out, and no more re-entering. That would safeguard the enterer if he safely entered for the first and the last time.

Abhi returned to his seat, energised enough to design his plans in a more refined manner. He had now to build a structure which would help him execute the job. He again started a new search on the internet and also checked his own rack of books for the relevant portions which he should keep in mind while designing the infrastructure. What he was planning was to introduce some software into Uday Singh's system which would remain embedded resting in his operating system. Whenever any activity was done by the system, the software would simply transmit the same through some network to an outside system without being touched by any of the electronic fences available on the system. He wanted to transmit the complete data to one of the systems under Rajal's control so that Rajal may use it as he required. Rajal would not be able to make any changes into the activities done by the host system, but would be able to record and play everything on his system. In a way, Abhi would create a read only mirror screen on Rajal's side for whatever activity was done on Uday Singh's system. Rajal would have all the information transmitted to him at his disposal, which he could use as he liked.

✦

Aditi's classes had ended; she was just winding up and checking all the PCs left on by her students. She had been thinking all day long of Rajal. She had been thinking of many plans. She even planned to go straight to Rajal and tell him that she had fallen in love with him and was ready to go into a physical relationship with him. But that would be too easy and may be if a person gets something easily, the value of it diminishes. Even if she had started having feelings for Rajal, she was not sure whether Rajal would also develop similar feelings towards her. He had wanted to have a relationship with her in the past, but what if he was interested in that one night stand only? What if he was already engaged with someone? There were still many 'ifs' which needed to be cleared, and for that, they had to meet more. This gave rise to another situation: how to plan these meetings. She just couldn't ask him out for coffee or dinner; they were not college buddies. Also she couldn't just bump into him in the market or anywhere he frequented. That would be ridiculous.

By evening, Aditi was still unsure as to how to approach him, with love or pure business. Business reminded her of her chat with Rajal in the coffee shop where there was a mention of her desire of starting a business of her own. Why not fix another meeting with Rajal on the pretext of taking her talk further and seeking Rajal's help in the same. Aditi looked at the clock in her room; it was 10:30 p.m. It was late but she had no choice; she had limited time in hand. Aditi dialled Rajal's number, but it remained unanswered. Maybe he was busy or asleep by then. She decided to call again in the morning.

✦

In another city Rajal was half lying in his bed sipping coffee when he saw his mobile phone vibrating. He saw Aditi's name flashing on it. A cruel smile floated on his lips and he silenced the phone, keeping it back on the side table. He looked at the wall clock in front, it was around 10:30 p.m. Rajal was tired and was not in a mood to talk to Aditi. He needed to have a fresh mind to talk to Aditi. Rajal started thinking how he had to drive faster to cover the time lost because of his rendezvous with Alka. He liked to be on time. They had reached by 3:30 p.m. and after getting dressed hurriedly they both headed straight to the award function hall. The function was yet to start as along with other guests, the chief guest had not arrived. Rajal and Alka were given their seat numbers at the reception and were shown to their seats by an escort.

The function started late by approximately one hour, but finished on time by six. Rajal had planned to drive back the same day, but now the plans had changed. Rajal started meeting other guests during the tea and involved himself in long conversations with them, even getting introduced to new people and developing new relations. By the time guests left and the party was over, it was already 8:00 p.m.

"Will we be able to drive back now? I think it's too late," said Alka, smiling and holding Rajal's hand while coming out of the hall into the open lawn of the resort.

"I think you should call your family to inform them that the weather is bad here and it will be difficult to drive down the hilly road at this time. We will leave early morning tomorrow," answered Rajal looking at the cloudy skies and enjoying the light drizzle on his face.

Alka took her phone out and called her husband. Having disconnected the phone, she looked at Rajal and said, "Now what? Are we going to wet ourselves or go inside?"

Rajal kissed her hands and pulled her inside the resort towards the main reception. Rajal booked two separate rooms and the usher escorted them to their respective rooms. In his room, Rajal washed his face and freshened up after the usher left. He then left his room and went towards the room just opposite and pressed the bell. The door was opened instantaneously. Standing at the door with her hair flowing all over her shoulders up to her chest, Alka was looking stunning and quite luscious. Rajal entered, closed the door behind him and simultaneously pulled Alka locking his lips with hers in a long, intoxicating kiss. Slowly keeping his lips locked with Alka's, Rajal started taking her towards the centre of the room and reaching close to the bed, he undraped and dropped her sari on the floor, his fingers unzipping her blouse while Alka had unbuttoned Rajal's shirt and took it off. While Rajal removed Alka's bra, they had to momentarily unlock their lips to pull out Rajal's vest through his head. Rajal on top of Alka, again locking their lips and taking out their other garments by themselves. They slid to the centre of the bed and plunged into the the final act. Feeling the thrust by Rajal, Alka groaned in ecstasy and after a few minutes of horseback pushes by Rajal, both simultaneously groaned louder and reached their orgasm.

Sipping his coffee, Rajal was recalling his evening with Alka. Rajal turned towards the other side where Alka was lying naked, sipping the last of the drops of coffee in her mug. Keeping her mug aside, she extended her hands again towards Rajal to embrace his bare body and merge with him once again.

✦

Having tried Rajal's number once without any luck, Aditi took the pillow in her embrace and lay down on her bed. Raghubir's threat haunted her every night which she tried to suppress by turning her thoughts towards thinking of ways to avoid it. Rajal would be her biggest saviour in the event if Abhi was not able to meet the deadline. She expected Rajal to become her saviour in both ways – financial, and if required, physical. But first, since financial help was what she had in mind, she wanted to work only towards that, while keeping other options open if it was required in future. Turning around in the bed and lying on her back, she began to imagine Rajal looking straight from above, slowly coming down to a distance of one nose away. Aditi moved her lips up to touch Rajal's and unknowingly, her hands started circling over her breasts pressing them hard. Aditi closed her eyes and gestured kissing Rajal's lips above her, pressing her breasts harder. She moved one of her hands further down to prepare for the bliss alone in the darkness of her own bedroom.

In the other room, Abhi had been working on a pen drive. He had opened it with a screwdriver and was soldering some points on it, wearing a magnifying telescopic eye on one of his eyes. About twenty pages of circuit diagrams were lying scattered on his table and four open books scattered over his bed with several portions marked with a highlighter or underlined with a red pen. Now and then, he plugged the chip through the USB port to his laptop and checked the calibrations. Once the hardware calibrations matched his requirement, he plugged in the pen drive to his laptop and started working on the soft part. Several logics had to be built, tested and refined. This had to work as a single shot gun and hence had to be hundred percent accurate, with no chance of a miss. If it failed the first time, there may not be a second attempt, and he would be doomed for life. Nothing traversed through his mind except the end result required through the logical flow of the software he was preparing. Somewhere in the silence he heard a groan, but his ears were immediately closed by his mind. His brain had silenced all his senses to concentrate only on the programme writing and strengthening the logic he was building. The night was still young for him, even though the city was well into the depth of its slumber.

9th Day

The morning was bright and pleasant, not because the atmosphere was different, but because most of the people had awakened fresh after having pleasant nightly activities. Rajal woke up naked besides an equally naked beautiful woman and immediately had quick morning sex. Abhi woke up to a possible solution to his impending problem of many days. Aditi woke up with a feeling of getting the most desired desire of her life. Alka got up with Rajal atop her for another orgasmic awakening.

Abhi had already prepared a prototype and now was the time to test the same in some foreign territory. If it became successful, the job would be done before time and liabilities would be paid off. Presently, there seemed to be no reason to foresee a failure; he had programmed it well, but any prototype cannot be declared a success unless it is tested in a real scenario. In the present project, the requirement of success percent was nothing less than cent percent. There were several scenarios where it could fail. The host system may not accept the software at all, it may accept but detect it as a malware and take action to eliminate it. If the software did get correctly placed undetected, then also it may not recognise the correct activity to be captured and could transmit incorrect data. If everything went well, it may still not get the connectivity between host and remote and lose important data. To get everything right, Abhi needed to test the same in a live scenario. He planned to put the bug in his own system at the office and try to transmit to his laptop at home. This would serve his purpose of checking the robustness of his office systems, to see whether it went undetected or was found. If caught, he would have to have a proper alibi.

Abhi's fingers were playing with the pen drive in his pocket which was an experimental piece and was to be used in testing the logic built by him. Working on his system in the office, Abhi's mind was wandering away again and again. When his colleagues started getting up for lunch and moved towards the pantry, Abhi stealthily brought out his pen drive covered in his palm and mounted it on the USB slot of his all-in-one PC. He had to escape the eyes of the camera installed in the office. Though there was no restriction in using USB devices, he didn't want to get noticed. As soon as his pen drive became active, the PC gave a message of a drive getting connected. Abhi waited, the system flashed for screening the pen drive for viruses. He accepted and clicked for the scan to start. In another few seconds, the scan was completed – no malware found. Abhi let out a sigh of relief; the software had passed its first test.

Abhi just locked his screen and, letting the pen drive stay attached, and moved away to have lunch, giving enough time to all the security systems and firewalls of their main server to try and detect what was embedded in the pen drive. During lunch, he remained as normal as he could, but internally he was preparing himself for a call from his server administrator of having detected a virus attack or some unidentified activity on his system. He was ready with his answer that it was a new pen drive and he had run a scan after connecting it. After lunch, he had coffee with no visible hurry and then went out for a smoke with Shashank. By the time he returned to his seat, it was almost forty-five minutes since the drive had been attached to the system. He unlocked the screen. It was just the plain screen, nothing else. Another testing had been successful.

Aditi had taken the day off; she had a lot of preparation to do. She had to get herself prepared physically for what she had prepared herself mentally. There are several occasions in life when a person unknowingly does the same thing which he is trying to avoid. Actually the underlying substance is the same, even if we try to change the outer appearance. Aditi was also trying to avoid the consequences she might have to face at the hands of Raghubhai's goons, but now had to plan something with the same end result. She feared that she would be made the scapegoat of some rowdy man's lust, but to avoid it, she was knowingly going to satisfy another man.

She got up late. As Abhi was leaving, she said she wasn't in the mood to go to office. Abhi did not question her as he seemed to be in a hurry to go to work. After Abhi left, she checked the yellow pages book for a good spa and got an appointment at one. She needed to get her body pampered and to make each of her pores emit a fragrance to excite not only the nasal senses of a man but his underlying testosterones. This would help her achieve her objective sooner. Thereafter, she fixed an appointment with her regular beauty clinic for a special treatment. She again gave a thought to her decision, to make herself understand that if she wanted to back, it was now or never. But she had no choice; backing out now would have grave consequences which she was not ready to accept. Also, what to do with her body was her own choice and not anyone else's. She got up and went straight to the washroom to have a good shower before going to the spa. A conversation with Rajal in the morning had confirmed a meeting that evening at the same coffee shop.

✦

Rajal, while driving back with Alka, was still thinking about how he needed to handle Aditi since he had already goofed up with her once. When Aditi called back in the morning, he was resting on his bed after having luscious early morning sex with Alka. Alka had gone to the washroom.

"Hello Aditi, so early in the morning, is everything fine?" asked Rajal as he picked up the call.

"Sorry to disturb you, but last night I gave a serious thought on the conversation we had last time about a business of my own, so I thought before I change my mind, I should tell someone who can push me if my impulse becomes weak. So I wanted to meet you and get your advice on the same," said Aditi in a short monologue.

"Ah sure, when?"

"Today evening when you are free?" said Aditi.

"Okay, let's meet at seven at the same cafe," said Rajal.

"Yeah fine. I will be there, and if there is any change of plan, do let me know. I know you are a busy man," Aditi said with a slight smile, trying to sound sensuous.

"Yeah sure, I will," assured Rajal.

"Okay then, see you in the evening and sorry again for disturbing you."

"Bye, see ya," said Rajal before disconnecting the phone, watching Alka come out of the bathroom, rubbing her naked body with a towel. He got up and went towards her. He clutched her moist hair with his hands and embracing her tightly put a deep kiss on her lips. Alka hugged him tightly. For a few minutes, time stood still. Slowly releasing her after a few minutes, Rajal went to the washroom to get fresh and get ready for his journey back home.

Thinking about the morning, Rajal had a smile on his lips, imagining Aditi's face and body in place of Alka's.

✦

After making sure his pen drive's programme was not getting scanned by the antivirus programmes and other firewall systems, Abhi confidently removed the drive and deposited it in his pocket. As per his programming, the malware should have taken some microseconds to get itself transferred from the pen drive to the hard coded system of the PC. By now, it must have started transmitting the information to cloud space which he had subscribed to. He took out his smartphone and logged in to his cloud space to check if any data had been transmitted; to his surprise, it was all there in a language which a layman could not understand, but he as a programmer could. What he needed now was a programme to download this data frequently from this cloud and present it in the same form as was visible on his PC. This would present a mirror image of all activities on his system to another system. This seemed to be the best way by which he could transmit all the required data without any further intervention from his side.

✦

Coming out of the spa, Aditi was already feeling refreshed and was tempted to bask in her own fragrance. She fell in love with her own body and prayed for the fragrance to stay intact till late night as assured by the massage woman. Her next stop was the beauty parlour where she wanted to get her long black tresses treated. Aditi sat down with a magazine to wait for her turn. Sitting on the chair, she instructed the beautician about how she wanted her hair to flow that evening, with a few strands cut short over her forehead, letting them slip over her face occasionally. Though her hair was emanating a soothing moist fragrance, she instructed the beautician to make them more fragrant. As the beautician started her preparation, Aditi looked at herself in the mirror. She smiled making a mischievous gesture with her eyes and murmuring to herself, "Gorgeous lady!"

After reaching the city, and dropping Alka at her house, Rajal went straight to his office and attended some important business that had been pending. He interacted with the other employees, congratulating them for winning the award for the organisation and gave a motivating speech. By the time he was done, it was already 6:30 p.m. It had been a tiring day, but not tiring enough to skip another exciting coffee rendezvous. Finishing all day's job, he swivelled his chair towards the window at his back and stretched his legs. At 7:00 p.m. he ordered a cup of coffee from the pantry. After the coffee arrived, he dialled Aditi's number on his mobile.

Aditi had reached home by 5:00 p.m. She dressed herself in a beautiful red ensemble, the colour of erotica. She reached the cafe five minutes before time and sat at a corner table from where she could look at the entrance. She began rehearsing her thoughts within. It was a very crucial meeting and her life depended on it. Each minute of the wait seemed like a year and the delay was making her nervous.

At 7:15, her mobile rang; it was Rajal.

"Where the hell is he calling from?" murmuring to herself, she picked up the call.

"Hi, where are you? I am waiting at the cafe," she said instantly.

"Oh, I just remembered about our meeting, so I thought I should call. My mistake I got busy with one of my important clients and it will take another hour or so. Can we reschedule this meeting to tomorrow and extend it to a dinner as an apology for today's goof up?" said Rajal without giving any chance to Aditi to cross question him or express any displeasure.

"Yeah, of course. Actually while I was waiting for you I gave a thought to my business idea and think I need to discuss it in greater detail and one coffee meeting would not be sufficient for that. I think your idea of dinner tomorrow is better. So we will meet tomorrow," said Aditi hiding her disappointment.

"Well then done for tomorrow. I will message you the venue. Now I must rush back to the meeting and I apologise again for today," said Rajal.

"No worries, see you tomorrow." Aditi disconnected the call. She felt like crying but then controlling herself she ordered a coffee to uplift her mood.

Rajal disconnected the call, closed his eyes and got lost in his thoughts of how he had been managing the events for the last few days and how he should carry things forward for the next few days. He realised that every game and business had its own inherent risks and these have to be managed as and when they surface. After a few minutes, he got up, took his belongings and left for his house. He was also amused at the way he had increased Aditi's anxiety level. This would help in the early ripening of their relationship.

✦

It had been more than a week since Abhi and Aditi had sat down together for breakfast or dinner. That evening, when Abhi entered, he realised Aditi was not yet home and since it seemed she would be late, he ordered for two pizzas over phone and went in to freshen up. By the time he changed and was clearing the table, the pizzas had arrived. Abhi left one pizza at the dining table and took one to his room. Having a hot cheesy aromatic pizza was highly satiating. For some time, enjoying the cheese flowing out of the pizza, he forgot the tension he had been living in for so many days. Finishing the pizza and disposing off the empty box, he returned to his room and to his thoughts. It was like he just returned to his stale house after a stroll in the woods. He switched on his laptop, engrossing himself in the world of logical diagrams and programming language.

Having left the taxi two blocks from her building, Aditi decided to walk towards her apartment. What could have happened to Rajal that he had forgotten about meeting her. That meant that she had not been able to make a lasting impression on him. But on second thoughts, how silly she was, thinking she had created an irresistible liking in just one meeting or by just a sensual photograph on Facebook. And yes, how could Rajal forget her reaction years back when she had taken a strict stand against his advances. Rajal must be taking extra precautions not forgetting her as one of his sour adventures, and had not yet reconciled to her. After so long, God knows if he was already engaged with someone, then maybe he would not be interested in her at all.

Aditi guessed Abhi was in his room working when she entered the house. Suddenly she remembered about dinner. Abhi had not called and she had not brought anything to eat. The she noticed the pizza box on the dinner table. Opening the box, she also checked the copy of the bill that mentioned two pizzas had been ordered. That meant Abhi had already had his dinner. That was fine as she was in no mood to talk to him. She took the pizza, warmed it and then locked herself in her room. She could still see a gorgeously beautiful young girl in the mirror. She once again smelled herself and was pleased with the fragrance of her body. The thought that Rajal didn't know what he had missed today consoled and cheered her a little. Lightening her mood, she sat on her study table and slowly had her pizza, enjoying each bite. She realised that the pizza had alleviated her sagging mood.

She had prepared so well for the planned meet and had made up her mind for something which she would never have agreed to in normal circumstances. She had been expecting a lot. The evening could have solved all her present problems and could have opened the doors to a new life with Rajal. The unexpected turn of events with nothing significant happening had suddenly brought out the fact that everything doesn't go as planned.

Aditi then forced her mind to think about the next day. At least everything was not over yet and she had a dinner to look forward to. Though now, to regain her confidence, she needed to lighten her mind and the best way in the darkness of her room was to release the mental darkness with the extreme lightness of an orgasm. Aditi lay down on her back and started visualizing Rajal thrusting himself on her and kissing her. The lips started shivering and she delved deep into visions of Rajal pressing her down, piercing into her and taking her flying into a world of extreme happiness.

Rajal had been lying on his chest in his bed, in deep sleep, dreaming of lying in between Alka on one side and an extremely beautiful lady with her face covered by her silky black hair on the other. In his dreams, he shifted away from Alka towards the other lady and plunged his face into the soft perfumed silkiness.

10th Day

The heavy rain the next morning made the weather pleasant for those who had the privilege of having their morning tea in their gardens or balconies. Rajal had nothing much to do in the morning after his regular fitness regime in his house gym, so he left early for office. He had nothing much to do in the office either, but was just excited about the future which he was planning to build for himself. For many years, despite his company's prestigious profile, he had been losing major projects to the rival company. The solutions created by his company had always been comparable in terms of rate and quality with the other companies, but somehow he always missed grabbing the project by a fraction. There must be a mole, similar to what he was planning now, who had been providing exact details of his proposals to his rival company.

A year or so back he had been able to crack one of the employees of his rival company Solution Informatics, but he had not been capable enough to break into the citadel of Uday Singh. Shashank had been working for him in Uday Singh's set-up, but the information provided by him had been superficial and not of much help to Rajal. But he still kept him on his payroll to use him if ever required.

Reaching office, he could smell the fresh omelette on the drawing table in his cabin; it had been laid out and served with bread, jam and juice just minutes before his arrival. Rajal decided to have his breakfast before starting his day. The day may be long, as there were several staff meetings he had to attend. He had to also have a video conference after lunch for all the engineers working on the site of their projects across the globe. In some of the countries, it may be midnight, while in some, mid-day. He usually didn't have meetings at odd hours, but this time, it was necessitated. He had to keep his team ready for the bigger projects which may come into their lap in the next few days.

After finishing breakfast, Rajal looked at his appointment schedule on his laptop screen and was satisfied with the day's activities lined up for him by his secretary. The one thing which he had himself lined up was already registered in his mind. He called Hotel Tulip's reception and booked a table for two for a candle light dinner at eight in the evening. In the next few seconds, he received his booking confirmation message from the hotel. He immediately forwarded the message to Aditi's number.

As Rajal was settling down, his secretary called to inform that Alka was there to meet him. Rajal asked her to be shown in and not to be disturbed. In another minute, Alka entered the room and sat on the chair in front of Rajal. She was the only project head whose project report he wanted to check personally, while with the rest, he would review over the phone. Alka started her presentation with all the details of different stages of the projects handled by her department. The report was not too long, as most of the projects were either near completion or had just started. After finishing the review in half an hour, Rajal stood up, took Alka to the door holding her hand. He grabbed her by pushing her back against the door and placed his hands across her waist up to the shoulder, lifting her lips to his. Alka also clutched Rajal tightly and reciprocated the kiss. They slowly released each other and leaving Alka standing at the door, Rajal moved back to his table. He turned towards Alka and wiping his lips with his right thumb said, "I think we should have snacks like these more often and plan a full dinner sometime as well."

"Yes of course," replied Alka as she turned to leave the cabin.

Rajal sat on his chair watching the door close behind Alka and thanked the day he had refused a glass cabin and opted for opaque walls.

Aditi wanted to visit the spa again, but then decided not to, as it would be too early to repeat the process. Moreover, she was still smelling nice. Also she was not sure whether the meeting would materialize. She just went normally to office, with a dejected look to feign weakness so that she could leave early. Never in her life had she faked illness to avoid office, but circumstances change all rules of life. But never earlier in life had such a situation arisen. Reaching office, she was able to garner enough empathy that when she asked to leave at 4:00 p.m., she was instantly relieved and even offered a drop home. But she said she'd take a taxi and thanked everyone for the concern shown.

Till 4:00 p.m., Abhi also remained busy, refining his official programme which was part of the project. Then he took a five minute break, shifting his attention to his clandestine programme where he had fixed nearly everything except a little concern on the continuous transmission of data as he knew there would be a break in network. If his programme was disconnected from the network, the intervening data in transit would get lost. The only solution he could arrive at was to first record everything on the same machine and then let the data transfer in a single shot whenever there was net connectivity and whatever data could not get transferred due to the connection issue could get initiated again on next availability of the connection. It would be similar to the filling of the overhead tank by a water pump motor from a filled water reservoir tank on the ground floor instead of the pump connecting directly to the water pipe line. This would rid the system of the extra pressure on the bandwidth and data could be transmitted whenever the bandwidth was available and system was visibly dormant. Having done some initial setup, Abhi winded up the day to go home and improvise on his theory.

Reaching home, Aditi took all the time to have a good bath with a perfumed body wash, rubbing each part of her body as if to fill each pore of her skin with perfume drops and emit fragrance forever. Massaging her body and then cleaning the foam with soft sprinkling water droplets falling like bliss on her tender parts, Aditi closed her eyes, enjoying the intoxicated feeling. Bathing had never been much fun before, nor had it been so intoxicating. Suddenly remembering the purpose of this bath, Aditi came out of her heavenly slumber and took quick stock of her body. Getting satisfied with the bath, Aditi wiped the extra water slowly, keeping the moisture intact.

Aditi went on to dry her conditioned hair and then caress them properly with the help of another exotically perfumed hair spray, making the hair shine glossily. Putting on her red dress again, she dressed herself elegantly, applying the matching make-up, brushing her cheeks, and matching nail paint both on fingernails and toenails. She had lost her own identity and had transformed herself into a doll desired by every male. She was now sure that every man passing by her would certainly turn his head. Aditi patted herself for this amazing show of her own self and congratulated herself for such a great transformation in her personality. She was fully confident that now, no one

could refuse her the attention she required and would not be in a position to say no to whatever she proposed, especially Rajal. She had called for a taxi. It would take around forty minutes for her to reach Hotel Tulip.

Opening the door of his flat, Abhi was greeted with a gush of perfume. Surprised, he entered the house to find some activity going on in Aditi's room. He thought he'd ask her, but then dropped the idea, not wanting to disturb her. It must be some wedding she'd be attending, thought Abhi. It also meant he had to order pizza again, but only for himself. Without disturbing Aditi, he quickly closed the door and went across to his room to prepare for another round of hectic brainstorming to develop the logic of his programme. He had very little time left and was still not sure if what he had been planning would work. If it didn't work, he didn't have enough time to plan afresh. He also didn't have any backup plan. This made Abhi restless as there was a higher chance of failure, which would bring dire consequences with it. For a person like him losing against musclemen of the society was not new, but this time it involved his family. He brushed aside the thought of failure and composed himself to concentrate.

Aditi looked at herself in the mirror, composed herself, took a deep breath and clutching her wallet, moved out of her room. Crossing the living room, she didn't notice Abhi's room lights and went out of the house locking the door behind her. She came down to the ground floor and noticed the cab waiting for her. The driver himself came across to open the rear passenger door, as if to welcome the queen in her royal ensemble.

✦

Rajal was playing with the keyboard of his desktop surfing some sites on the net, while Alka was sitting in front of him detailing about a glitch which had come across in one of their projects being run at an overseas location. Rajal had no serious interest in the glitch being explained to him, nor was he surfing anything important. He was just watching the time flashing on the screen at the bottom right hand corner. It was already 7:30 p.m. and he was calculating the time he would take to reach the hotel. He was amused to see how Alka took every opportunity to visit him in his cabin. Before her joint visit to the award ceremony, Alka used to come to Rajal's cabin only when it was important and that was usually once or twice a month. They usually used to communicate over phone or email. Since morning, she had already visited him four times. It was as if she was a teenager again and wanted to see and smell him again and again. Guessing that Rajal was not listening to whatever she was saying, she got up, went around the table, turned Rajal's chair away from his table and seated herself on his lap. She lifted his face and planted a long kiss on Rajal's lips. Kissing Rajal passionately for the next minute or two, Alka got up, straightened her dress and moved towards the door, giving him a flying goodnight kiss again. Rajal also gestured a flying kiss as the cabin door closed behind Alka. It was 7:45 p.m. when Rajal shut down the screen.

As Aditi came out of the taxi at the hotel's drive in, she could see Rajal sitting on the driver's seat of the car just behind her taxi. Rajal wished her with a flick of his neck and drove in towards the waiting valet. He walked up to Aditi and said, "I thought I was getting late, but you saved me from the embarrassment."

"Yes, I think we both saved each other from getting late," said Aditi blushing.

"Shall we ..." gestured Rajal to Aditi to come along inside.

At the restaurant, they were shown to their table in a secluded corner. As soon as they sat facing each other, Rajal had a good look at Aditi and instantly realised that the extraordinarily

stunning beauty sitting across him had prepared specially for this occasion. His delaying tactic had made her work more sincerely towards this meeting.

"It's a good place, quiet and serene," said Aditi looking around, also noticing Rajal gazing at her.

"Ah yes, a good place. Someone had recommended it to me earlier, so I thought we should try it," said Rajal, hiding the fact that he had been to the place many times earlier.

"Well, how's life going? It seems there has been some thinking going on during the last few days,"asked Rajal.

"Thinking! Yes, you may say so. Actually after our last meeting, the thought of doing my own business started making way into my mind and then several ideas started floating," said Aditi.

"Well, let's first order some soup and then decide what to have for dinner," interrupted Rajal as he waved to the waiter.

By the time soup arrived, both had decided on the dinner items which was then ordered. Having a sip of his hot chicken soup, Rajal started again, "So what have you been thinking?"

"Something which I can enjoy doing and carry forward even if I face some initial setback. Something where I have the skills to bring things back on track if it gets derailed," said Aditi, thinking how to turn the discussion towards what she was really there for.

"So what would that be? Opening an institute because that is what you are good at ... teaching," suggested Rajal.

"May be, as you said, I am good at teaching," agreed Aditi.

"Well thought. You can open a teaching institute for vocational teaching. People nowadays flock to any place teaching computing, it's an IT age and no one wants to be left behind," said Rajal.

"Hmm ..." murmured Aditi sipping her soup. "But what do you think will be required to start it? A place to open the institute, hardware, then basic teaching materials?"

"Yes, the white or black boards, chairs, computers and some more teachers, an affiliation and much more," explained Rajal further.

"Oh yes, I forgot the affiliation part. Without it, no one will join the institute," exclaimed Aditi.

"Yes, of course, no one will even look at the sign board without the affiliation part written on it," laughed Rajal lightly.

"What do you think will all this cost, I don't have any idea of the market rate of acquiring all of this," said Aditi, slightly bewildered.

"There are some legal costs and then there are some illegal costs to get things done legally."

"How so, I don't understand."

"Well, for the affiliation part, you need to pay the fees of application and other such affiliation related documentation and charges, which is a legal cost. But apart from this, you need to pay some other individuals to grant such an affiliation, which will be the illegal cost," explained Rajal.

"But why to individuals? Doesn't the legal cost cover their charges too?" asked Aditi.

"Besides paying all the legal charges, there will still be some individuals who will be involved in granting such an affiliation and they need their portion also. And yes, now don't say that they already get their salary for this job, because this doesn't matter," further explained Rajal.

"But that is corruption!"

"Of course that is corruption!"

During the discussion they had already finished their soup and were now being served their dinner.

"I don't know how I will do all these things. Can you guess what will be the amount that will be required for starting this type of venture?" Aditi enquired more deeply.

Rajal looked at Aditi again as she was lifting the spoon towards her juicy lips and pulling back the strands of hair falling on her cheeks to the back of her ear lobe with the other hand. After putting the bite into her mouth, Aditi glanced towards Rajal and felt a little shy on seeing Rajal gazing at her. Rajal then spoke as if after a long calculation, "I think something around fifty lakhs will be a decent amount to start with."

"Fifty lakhs!" exclaimed Aditi. "It's too large an amount. I am already in a fix for which it is difficult to arrange and now another fifty lakh, pheww … Life is too harsh."

"Why what fix are you in now?" wondered Rajal.

"Oh nothing, there is some personal liability for which I may need to arrange some odd twenty lakhs within this week and now you estimate another fifty. Really the world is becoming too costly to live in," said Aditi, rushing her brain cells to mould the discussion towards what she had actually wanted to bring out.

"The world is costly, but not for those who have the courage to face what life throws at them," consoled Rajal. "And yes, those who want to do something can go to any extent to get that."

"So what do I do to go all out to arrange for this large an amount of funds? I think this amount will take another two hundred years for me to amass, and by that time the requirement will increase by that many number of times," said Aditi desperately.

"Well, not so. It's just a matter of breaking our mental barrier. If you want, you can earn that much money in just no time," said Rajal casually.

And this was the sentence which gave Aditi the opportunity; thinking fast, she shot her master stroke, "So are you offering me the same deal which you offered two years back?" questioned Aditi, seemingly arrogant, stopping in the middle of the dinner.

"Oh no … no, I didn't mean that. You see, what I was trying to say …" Rajal acted embarrassed, not sure how Aditi would take it.

Aditi raised her palm towards Rajal's face gesturing to him to keep quiet, looking into Rajal's eyes for a few seconds, then lowering her hand slowly and putting another spoon in her mouth. "On second thoughts, I think if I do get a deal like that today, I may accept it since times have changed."

Rajal smiled at what Aditi just said and looked across. She seemed to be quite at ease. Both continued with their dinner silently for the next few seconds without looking at each other. Aditi had butterflies in her stomach, while Rajal was thinking how sensuously beautiful Aditi was looking and was getting excited smelling her fragrance along with a sense of an opportunity.

After a while, Rajal spoke, "Are you proposing to me now?"

"No, but checking on the validity of the proposal you put forward a couple of years ago … if it's still within its expiry date?" said Aditi blushing and wondering how she was able to say everything so clearly.

"Times have changed, you see, and I regret the mistake I made that day," said Rajal apologetically. "But on second thoughts, I am still interested in the proposal as it has not yet expired," said Rajal slowly, giving extra weight to each word. He had his eyes fixed on Aditi, piercing through her eyes, trying to gauge the effect of his words. Aditi was also looking straight into his eyes. Gathering all her courage, taking a final decision inside her, she opened up. "Do you think twenty lakhs would be too much for the deal?"

Looking at the silky black hair flowing over her shoulders, Rajal smilingly said, "I don't think so. If you are a part of this deal, it would be value for money."

Aditi having got a positive response felt relaxed and was able to see her problem coming to an end soon. "But it should not be just for one meeting. We should go for a complete experience and enjoy it completely. After all, it is a once in a lifetime deal," said Rajal.

"I am in a little hurry and need the money urgently," said Aditi, fearing that she may have to face exploitation and should limit it to the minimum. Rajal correctly guessing the same came up more openly, "Oh come on! Just some days of enjoyment. Maybe a week."

Calculating the days already elapsed and those she had in hand, Aditi said, "What is your plan? Can we be more open now and discuss the modalities of the deal clearly.

"O ...O ... you have already become a good business person. Well, I think we should plan a vacation somewhere for a week ... a full week of togetherness," explained Rajal.

"A week! And where to?" asked Aditi.

"Well, if you agree, then I will plan that by tomorrow," said Rajal finishing his last bite and picking up the napkin.

"And when will I get my dues?"

"The day we return."

"In cash?"

"Yes, full in cash."

"Do I have reason to believe you will not go back on your word?"

"I am a good businessman and will never cheat a business partner with whom I will be doing business again."

"But this one week rendezvous will cost twenty-five lakhs then," said Aditi, calculating how she might have to spend to recuperate from the week. Surrendering to a man to have sex for money is something which is culturally not taken well in the society she lives in. These society rules get imprinted on one's own emotional self and would be hard to erase. It will be a permanent scar on her soft senses and will also be a deciding factor in her life. It had to be compensated accordingly. Now that she had already gone ahead with her plan of selling herself in a sophisticated way, the price must be right.

"Okay, that's fine with me. We can plan it sometime next month. I have some urgent errands to be completed in the next fifteen days, then we can surely have our piece of this world somewhere away from this world," said Rajal.

Next month would be too late, thought Aditi. It would have to be that week. Now that she had taken the plunge, why fear the chill. Yet, she could not show her eagerness, and she still was not a whore.

"Yeah, that would be fine, but I am in urgent need of some money by next week. Can you lend me some till next month?" pitched Aditi.

"Well, if that is so, I can make some arrangements this week itself for our outing, but then I can arrange for twenty lakhs only, as I will also have to postpone some of my arrangements which will incur some cash outflows," replied Rajal.

So Rajal was a good businessman and even in such deals he didn't forget to bargain. How shrewd, thought Aditi, but she had no choice. Her position was weaker at present.

"Well, it's better than postponing it till next month. Now by when can you give me the details as I need to take leave from my job," Aditi asked.

"I will inform you by tomorrow after getting all the arrangements done."

Having already finished the dinner, both got up to move out. While Aditi was walking ahead, Rajal was all appreciative of the perfectly curved body swaying delicately in front of him. This was the body he had been longing for and sighed at the thought of holding this body in his clutches in a few days. He offered to drop Aditi home, to which she readily agreed. Rajal drove towards her house getting directions from Aditi. He dropped her in front of her apartment building and sped away.

While finishing his pizza, Abhi heard the main door click. He guessed it was Aditi back from her party. He focussed his attention towards the flowchart he had been working on. Building a reservoir within the system itself had its own shortcomings: it may get detected easily, it may slow down the system, forcing the user to investigate the reason for the slowness. It was also difficult to hide the memory used in occupying the reservoir area. Several ideas were coming into his mind, but each was riskier than the other. Thinking over and over the sole idea which came to him was to attach a separate memory which could be camouflaged in the original hard disk without giving the system any extra space, nor occupying any space on the original system memory. This would never attract the attention of the user to anything abnormal being noticed. But for this idea, he needed at least one chance to open the processor portion of the system since this required a hard installation of some hardware. The idea was workable, but with less chance of getting an opportunity to implement it, which left him with the option of keeping both types of system architecture ready and use the one which got a chance to be implemented – one without adding memory space, and another by adding the memory and camouflaging it. Abhi started working on the first option since he needed some more research and planning for the other option. He also needed to search the market for the type of hardware he would require. Time was short and he had to get at least one of the options ready to start with as it also required physical access to the targeted system.

While Abhi was still working on his prototype, Aditi's room dipped into darkness and the body had called it a day with much more satisfaction. The plan was on its correct path, and just needed some course correction to achieve desired results. As the night entered its darkest hour, Abhi's room was still lit while he had already fallen into deep sleep sitting on his chair with his hand down on the table across him where his laptop was still working on the commands given to it.

*

11th Day

It had been three days since Rajal had explained the job to Abhi, but till then had got no news from him. He had seemed to be in a big hurry, but now there was no news of the progress. This was making Rajal a bit concerned, even though Rajal was sure Abhi was not a person who would just quit. Rajal was engrossed in these thoughts when his aide informed him of Alka's arrival to meet him. Smiling, Rajal thought of the rendezvous with Aditi the previous night and then his earlier escapades with Alka. He pulled himself up and opened one of his mails on the laptop to look busy.

Alka entered the cabin wishing Rajal a good morning. Looking up at Alka, he felt refreshed again. She was dressed in a light blue sari with her wet and left loose over-flowing hair falling on one shoulder and the other shoulder exposed with a sleeveless blouse clinging on to it. Having gauged Alka's beauty in a few seconds, he greeted her with a smile and lifted his eyebrow appreciating Alka's get-up which made Alka blush.

✦

At another office, Abhi was busy on his system, with all his concentration on the job he had in hand, his official one. The complete project had already been delayed and his unit had been subjected to a weekly review on the progress. Due to his personal engagements for the last couple of days, there had not been much progress in his part of the job. There was a review impending after two days where he had to state the progress and assure his seniors that he was now nearer to the completion of his part. Abhi thought of generating some queries related to his part of the program which would be sent to the client for clarifications, and that would be a good explanation for the slow progress of his work. Moreover, he had to spend some time on researching for the right kind of hardware for his other job, which was a priority for him at present.

Having finished her classes, Aditi was feeling stressed out with her days's job and decided to go to the bar and chill out. She had never been to a bar alone, so she felt a little awkward while entering the bar. She went in straight to the bar counter and seated herself on a high chair. Having ordered a beer for herself, she looked around to see if any known faces were around. As usual, there were groups of girls and boys partying around and some gyrating to the music on the dance floor. The barman placed a beer mug and a plate of roasted peanuts in front of her. She took a sip and turned her chair towards the dance floor. Suddenly the woman sitting on the chair beside her also turned and they both looked at each other, recognising and then greeting each other in surprise. She was Aditi's college friend's elder sister. She was alone as well. They decided to take a separate table and order another bottle of beer and talk about the old days. She was five years senior to Aditi, but since she was the elder sister of her best friend since school days, they had also developed a good friendship among themselves.

It had been ten days since his men had threatened Abhi, but there had been no news of further progress. Raghubhai was reminded of it when he looked at the calendar where he had marked the date when he had to approach Abhi for his money. Was he arranging for the money or would he be required to do what he had never done before – pick up a girl! Raghu may have been involved in several activities which could be legally categorised as crime, but he had never hurt a woman. This time as well, if it had not been for the Boss, he would not have asked his men to haul threats in the name of a girl. He didn't want to do it, but couldn't say no to the Boss. He was not sure how Abhi would return the money, and if he could not, then what would he have to do to the girl. He was getting scared at the thought of it. Raghu wanted to call Abhi and check if he was arranging for the same, but he could not without consulting his Boss, who had specifically asked him not to do anything until he was instructed to do so. Raghu dialled on the number saved as 'Boss'.

"Boss, it has been ten days since we issued a warning to Abhi. Shall I check if he is arranging to meet the deadline?"

Before he could explain anything further, he had to shut his mouth to listen to the Boss giving him a piece of his mind.

"Okay Boss, as you say. I will do nothing for now," he said timidly as he disconnected the call.

◆

"What are you so immersed in that you haven't been interacting with us during lunch or after office?" complained Shashank coming to Abhi's workstation and patting him on his back.

Abhi turned towards Shashank startled, "Oh nothing, just that we are already behind schedule. I was utilizing all the available time on resolving the issues in the programme."

"Okay, so it is the job pressure. I thought you had found a girlfriend," said Shashank laughing.

"Nothing of that sort. I don't have time to get involved in these types of activities and moreover, it's not me who will get a girlfriend, it's for a girl to make me her boyfriend, then only something of this sort will materialise," replied Abhi humorously.

"Well then, what's the agenda? Have you fixed the 'D' section?" asked Shashank.

"D-section, oh no. I am still stuck in the 'C' and there are some issues on which I need the client's clarification. I was just preparing the query sheet."

"Oh buddy, then you're way behind. Many of us have already started on 'E'. This week's review would be difficult for you. Be prepared or get something done in the next two days," said Shashank.

"Yeah I know, but I will manage. Just one more week and I will be online," replied Abhi.

"Well then, I will leave you alone, man."

"Ya see you," said Abhi to the departing Shashank who was going to have a smoke outside.

Shashank waved back and went out of the room. Going to the ground floor, at the cigarette shop on the opposite side of the road, he lit his cigarette. Pulling out his cell phone he dialled a number, "I think he is onto something, which may mean he is doing something else apart from his official work, otherwise why is he stuck on a part which has already been completed by some lesser talented colleagues of his," explained Shashank in detail.

He then listened for some time. The other voice passed some more instructions while also giving him the details of the payment Shashank was to receive. Taking down the instructions, Shashank felt ecstatic hearing about his payment details.

Abhi had again focussed on preparing the client query sheet and doing some more work on his system to complete the 'C' section as early as possible. Simultaneously, he kept the search engine page opened to keep studying the storage hardware architecture of a computer as well as for the other externally attachable storage options. He was more interested in a miniature circuit based storage option similar to micro SD cards used in mobile sets. He also needed the host plugs to attach such miniature storages to the laptop internally, and that also in a hidden way. His twin handling of both office and his personal jobs was making it difficult to complete either. Time was short for both, and without completion, none would be of any use. He was a man who could create magic sitting on his desk and playing with logic, but was poor with hardware. Even after arranging for all the hardware and perfecting his software, he had to plan for its physical implementation which was to be a difficult manoeuvre. But for now, he needed to complete everything in the next two days at the most. But within these two days, he was also required to complete the C section of his official project. In order to concentrate on his present official job, he closed the other search engine and continued to recheck his present assignment.

✦

It was not difficult for Rajal to arrange for a holiday home at a secluded location. It was a place on the outskirts of a nearby city and would take five hours to reach. Rajal had stayed in these homes twice earlier and had spent quality time for few days with his other female partners over the last few years. It was located in the middle of a forested area. The homes were well stocked. They were made ready for the people a day before their arrival and were cleared again after the guests left. Having finalised the arrangements, Rajal prepared an SMS detailing only the day and time he would pick her from her apartment building's gate and when he'd drop her back, and sent to Aditi's mobile number. He then pulled out his chequebook and wrote a cheque for twenty-five lakhs. He called his assistant and handing over the cheque asked the amount to be withdrawn from the bank on the ground floor of the same building. He continued checking his mails. One of the mails he had marked important was related to one of the upcoming projects for which bid invitation was to open the next week. This was the project which would give him a clear profit of at least twenty to thirty crores, for which he was already investing twenty lakhs through Abhi. The bagging of this project would also give him enough leverage to be able to spend another twenty lakhs on his long-awaited and highly desirable enjoyment week. His assistant brought the money in the next half an hour which he stuffed inside his laptop bag. While he was reviewing the steps of his plan, he got a call on his mobile which gave him some comforting news on his project running in the right direction. He felt relaxed after disconnecting the call from Shashank, promising to give him a bonus apart from the regular payment.

◆

Reaching home late, Abhi saw that dinner had been kept ready on the dining table. Aditi's room lights were switched off. She might have gone to sleep. It was better that they had not met the last few days or else she may have guessed that he was in some trouble and then it would have been difficult to explain things to her. Closing the door of his room, Abhi again started the search engine on his laptop to search for a miniature storage device. Several sites came up for this search, after going through some of the sites which detailed on the research going on in miniature storage devices, he zeroed in on some sites where some such devices were on sale. There was a device which was half a centimetre by one third of a centimetre and claimed a storage of 128 GB. It also had an attachment to connect it to a USB port as well as an attachment to connect it to a serial port inside the laptop's spare port attached to the motherboard.

This was what he wanted. Something that could be connected inside with the motherboard of the system directly and remain undetected from the outside. This would be used to store the activities done on the system and then would empty itself by transferring all the stored data to the recipient system. There was no guarantee about how many hours or days it would work, but once a storage device is plugged in and is never removed, it usually works till infinity. He immediately placed an order for the same along with its attachments, choosing the option of express delivery. He now needed to devise a plan to approach Uday Singh's laptop.

Abhi then returned to his programming and started running some checks to check the efficiency of recognition and execution of commands by his programme. For another hour, his programme underwent several tests and attacks from its programmer and proved its mettle at every challenge thrown at it. Abhi was pleased to experience the efficacy of the programme designed by him. Thereafter, once satisfied, he switched off the system as well as the room lights and went to bed. Even after closing his eyes, his mind was keeping him awake, thinking on ways to approach the host system and plant his bug unnoticed. How to get through to the MD of the organisation was a big question for an employee like him, who was a much lower rung official in the hierarchy of the organisation. Finally, exhaustion took over his brain and shut it down, covering it in deep sleep, and letting the subconscious and unconscious parts of his brain start the healing process for the rest of the night.

✦

The breeze was cool, signalling rain drops being on the way somewhere waiting to fall on Aditi's face. She closed her eyes facing the sky, letting the breeze hit her face with its pace doubled by the speeding open sunroof of the car she was travelling in on the picturesque road spiralling through the hilly road. The smell of soaked earth and moist greenway enveloping the entire mountain was making the whole environment highly romantic. Suddenly, she felt fingers running through her hair and a warm breath over her neck. She opened her eyes to find Rajal diving his face into her dark and dense cascade of softness, with his lips brushing up her neck towards her ear lobes, while holding the steering wheel of the car with his right hand. Aditi rebuked him playfully and asked him to keep his eyes on the road. Rajal smiled at her, straightened himself, but simultaneously pulled Aditi's face towards his and planted a passionate kiss on her. The weather, the breeze, the drive, the landscape, all melted into an enchanting kiss. It took her out of this world into an unknown bliss she had never ever experienced before. Aditi opened her eyes again to take in the complete ecstasy of the intoxication. She wanted this to continue for eternity. For how long they both remained lost in their divine kiss, she did not know. Then slowly their lips detached and Rajal turned his attention towards the road ahead while Aditi leaned towards Rajal's shoulder and remained glued there.

When Rajal held her chin and lifted her face towards his, only then did Aditi realise that their car had stopped and may be they had reached their destination. She keenly watched Rajal getting down and coming around to her side, opening the door and extending his hand. Aditi extended her left hand and stepped out. Rajal closed the door of the car and kissed on the back of Aditi's palm. He then stooped down and lifted a surprised Aditi into his arms. She hid her face in Rajal's chest.

Entering the house, crossing the living room, he went straight to the bedroom. He placed Aditi gently on the bed. He slowly slid his hand from her knees through her thighs, travelling through her waist towards her bulging chest and up to her cheeks to remove the lock of hair covering her face. While he removed the strand of hair, Aditi opened her eyes. Seeing Rajal just inches above her face, she held his neck and pulled him in to join his tempting lips with hers again.

The supreme ecstasy felt by Aditi made her forget the dimensions of time, space and location. It was as if the whole cosmos was falling into pieces around them, having no meaning or value for that moment. Having immersed herself completely into Rajal, Aditi felt the stinging pain of Rajal coming into her, but then in a split of a second, it turned into a higher level of ecstasy. With her eyes closed, Aditi started taking in all the pushes Rajal was forcing and the infinite rubbing of her vaginal walls creating an out of the world feeling. When she finally drained herself out in orgasmic pleasure, with Rajal also slowing down in a few seconds of supreme bliss, she slowly released Rajal and opened her eyes to a deep dark brown room with the moonlight peering through one of the windows behind the curtains.

Aditi sat up on her bed. It was three in the night and despite the air conditioner on its optimum temperature, she felt sweat on her face and chest. Aditi got up and went to the washroom. She had a glass of water and tried to remember the experience. She looked around to find herself alone in her own room, and reassuring herself that it had been a dream, she again slipped back into the bed, trying to re-enter the same experience once again and letting the night give way to the days coming ahead.

12ᵗʰ Day

Rajal took deep breaths, inhaling the fresh air before stepping out on the street for a jog. He was usually accustomed to a run on a treadmill in his home gym, but that day he woke up early as sleep had broken away from his eyes. There seemed to be some excitement brewing inside him which was keeping him away from sound sleep. Was it due to the realization that he may succeed in beating his business opponents or was it the closeness to achieve one of his long awaited desires. Rajal thought about Aditi only while he passed many couples jogging. He smiled thinking of his plans for the next few days.

✦

Aditi was watching a couple walking on the grass barefoot, holding each other's hands and talking to each other. She herself was walking barefoot on the moist morning grass trying to feel the freshness. Aditi was feeling cold and moist from the inside; she wasn't feeling fresh. She needed some more fresh air to breathe in. Walking around the park for half an hour, she decided to sit down for a while and clear her mind. Sitting on the side bench in the open air, her thoughts started encircling her. What she was going to do was something absolutely unacceptable in her society. She was supposed to preserve her virginity for the one who would marry her. She was going to do something against the rules of the society and though it was going to be done in total secrecy, what if it got disclosed? Would she be able to handle it? She had sold herself to have sex with a rich man to earn money, then what was the difference between her and a professional? This is what she wanted to avoid happening to her in the hands of goons of Raghubhai and now the solution which she had found to save herself involved the same act with a different person in a different setting.

The sun was starting to emerge from the horizon and Aditi was still engrossed in her thoughts over her situation. The things that would directly impact her would be her own physical state of losing her virginity, her mental state of having felt the joy of orgasm, her need for money, her guilt of having resorted to this method of earning, her own eagerness to again long for this enjoyment having once tasted it, the feeling of being a criminal who had broken a social norm, one who has betrayed the confidence of her parents, her own image of a strong character getting shattered, her own years of contemplation of a sagely life getting ruined or she herself changing from one Aditi to a totally different Aditi. All of this in a single incident was making her rethink her decision over and over again. Now being so close to achieving her goal, she was still not sure whether to go for it.

Looking across the park, watching people walk and exercise in different postures, gave her one more confidence that everyone lived his life in a way different from other, but still they had same purpose of leading their life in a better way. Similarly, she also had the right to live life in a better way, however different the method might be. She was responsible for all her acts and their consequences. If she wanted to get what she desired, then she had the right to choose the methods.

Aditi had to meet her friend's sister on her way to office to receive something she had promised on the day they had met in the bar. This delayed her a bit, but by the time she reached office, much of her dilemma had already gone and she had some new thoughts to think upon. Relaxing with her head stretched above her chair with her eyes closed, she tried to imagine her future, which seemed changed now.

It seemed to be a day of confusion as another mind was also beginning to have some thoughts on the ethics of doing what he was planning to do. Abhi's mind was also in a dither over the question of right or wrong, loyalty and bigotry, responsibility and guilt. He was going to deceive his own company. He was going to be termed a traitor, if not by others, then by himself. What if he got caught? It may also happen that his contractor may use his services in the future as well. Would he be able to forgive himself for this act of deception? He had both Raghubhai and Uday Singh standing in front of him – one with a threatening finger and the other accusing him of this act of deception. Which of the two would be more difficult to handle? Sometimes he felt like talking to Uday Singh and disclosing Rajal's plans, but would it be of any use? Uday Singh was not going to take it delightfully and instead would lose the opportunity of earning money in such a short time.

At the same time, thinking again from a different viewpoint, it was pure business and not a sin. This act required a lot of talent and the urge to use that talent for activities like these. Moreover, an act which is wrong in one's eyes may stand good in another's; eyes or the same act may be good or bad, right or wrong in different situations. It is not the act which is bad, but the ultimate use of the act which terms it good or bad. For Uday Singh, it would be an act of deceit, while the same act would be highly appreciated by Rajal and worthy of a reward. He had to convince himself on the purpose of the act which would justify whether it was good or bad. Treachery is not only against national interest, but it is an act which betrays the expected behaviour of one against the other person, organisation, society or situation. Abhi's running away, leaving his sister in trouble, was more than treachery; it was murder of his own values and blood bonding. It was a betrayal of the vow that he gave his sister every Rakshbandhan and Bhaidooj. Howsoever much he tried to justify it, the point was that it was the requirement which justified the means. Today his requirement was to earn money in a limited time, because along with him, his sister was also at stake. Self concern was the major driver to make him sell out his own company. There was no time to think again or back out. There was no option now and this entire dilemma between good and bad had to be brushed aside.

✦

According to Rajal's plan, they had to leave the next day and it was a six-hour drive to their destination. Rajal had planned to drive himself as he didn't want any third person between him and Aditi. He still remembered the day when Aditi had rebuked him for bringing up a seemingly unacceptable proposal to her. During these years, he had learnt and mastered the tricks of the trade. He believed he could draw any woman towards himself. Having mastered the act of seduction, he was never sure whether Aditi could be lured easily. It had been difficult with Aditi, but after all, he had managed to capture her and now his long awaited desire was going to be fulfilled. As Rajal was deeply contemplating on his future actions, his cell rang. Looking at the screen, he could see Aditi's number flashing. Smiling, he picked up the call.

Aditi talked to Rajal with a lot of conviction and got him to agree to cancel the outdoor trip and instead plan something within the city itself. She had to fake the unexpected arrival of her parents which would make it impossible for her to go out with him on a vacation outside the city. She had to convince Rajal to arrange for a secluded place within the city itself where they both could hole up and enjoy. Having got a confirmation from Rajal about re-planning their rendezvous, she called a friend and discussed a few things before returning to her work. Though Aditi had got the plans changed for the time being, she also had the fear of her plans going completely awry. She had taken a calculated risk, but the fear of failure had also trickled in.

Rajal was equally uncomfortable with this change of plan. What is it that Aditi was planning? It was not easily understandable, but her stupid excuse made him guess that Aditi was still not completely comfortable with the arrangement and was buying time. But did she have time enough to take the liberty of postponing the predetermined arrangements? Rajal had accepted her excuse to give her the required time and also the mental freedom as he knew Aditi's requirement would force her to accelerate the commitment with him. He just needed to have patience and wait for the right time. Rajal dialled his relationship manager at his regular hotel and got his regular suite booked for this complete week.

✦

Abhi left his office early as he had to move out of his comfort zone of soft programming to the hard world of machines. He had already ordered the storage device, but there was one component he needed to design himself which would make him enter that system which was to be bugged. Abhi went to a well-known electronics market of the city, where one could find the smallest of the chips to the largest of the printers or photocopiers. It had everything from the spurious to original.

Abhi walked around and picked up some items which he had planned, and as per availability of parts, had to change the configuration of his prototype on the spot. Satisfied with the parts he had purchased, he returned home by 9:00 p.m. and found Aditi in the kitchen making dinner. It would be after one entire week that both of them would be having home-made dinner together. Abhi kept his belongings in his room and came back to help Aditi.

Both of them had dinner and exchanged some of their office gossip, primarily events related to their commonly known friends. Talking to each other after such a long time refreshed them a lot. After dinner, both bid good night to each other and went to their respective rooms. Sitting on his bed, Abhi opened the packets he had brought to check all the parts and started arranging them in proper order to make the gadget he had in mind. After approximately fifteen minutes, Aditi knocked on the door and came in with a cup of coffee.

"Here, have some coffee! I think you have been working late for the last few days. Don't take too much stress ... everything will be fine," consoled Aditi.

Aditi kept the coffee mug on the table and walked out, closing the door of Abhi's room. She sat in the drawing room with a magazine, sipping her own coffee. Abhi read the diagram again and plugged in the soldering machine. While sipping his coffee, he studied the diagram and looked at the parts. He seemed satisfied that he would be able to complete one major part of his big job. While he finished half of his coffee, he started feeling a little drowsy and hence sat on the edge of his bed adjoining his study table. He slowly moved his eyes towards the diagram and the parts on the table. It seemed that the world was moving in slow motion and then he felt as if his hands were picking up the parts and joining them in the similar way as was portrayed in the diagram. He kept watching himself doing the job in an animated way and then slowly closed his eyes, still feeling the pressure of completing the act as per the diagram.

Finishing her coffee, Aditi moved her eyes from the magazine towards Abhi's room. The lights were still on. She got up to wish him goodnight. As she opened the door, she saw Abhi half lying on his bed with his eyes closed, legs still hanging out of the bed, lips murmuring something and his hands moving. Aditi smiled and stepping inside the room, placed Abhi's legs properly on the bed, and made him lie on his back. When Aditi was switching off the lights before leaving, she again looked at Abhi and was amused to see he was still dreaming with his eyes closed, his fingers moving. She was pleased to see the effect of just a few drops of the drug she had mixed in Abhi's coffee in order to check the results as promised by her friend. She went to her room and remembered her friend telling her that the drug would not only overpower a man's senses with sleepy unconsciousness, but also make him feel that he was doing the job which he had been thinking of the most while getting sleepy. It would make him feel as if he was actually doing the act which he was planning to while the drug was taking effect. She was happy to see the effect of the drug on her brother.

13th Day

Abhi opened his eyes feeling a little dizzy. He felt amazed at waking up with a mixed feeling of lethargy and vigour simultaneously. He got up and as he came out of the bed straightening himself, he glimpsed at his study table. The drawing was lying on it as it is and the electronic parts were also scattered all over. As far as he remembered, he had made the device in the night before going to sleep. Did he dismantle it before sleeping? But why would he do that? It was beyond his understanding. He was absolutely sure he had prepared the device with his own hands but could not remember when he had uninstalled the items again. Had he been sleep walking? Did he do it in his sleep which he now could not remember? But this had never happened earlier. In his confused state, Abhi completed his morning chores and tried hard to remember the events of the night after he had assembled the device. When he got ready, Abhi collected all the items on the table and stacked them into one of the drawers. Now he had to build the device again. There was going to be a delay of one more day.

As Abhi came into the living room, he saw Aditi having her breakfast. She was up early for a Sunday. He greeted Aditi and sat on the adjoining chair. Aditi looked amusedly at her brother's baffled face and asked, "What happened? Is everything fine?"

"Yes, everything fine, just a little confused," answered Abhi, with a bite of bread in his mouth.

"What confusion, something important?"

"Nah, nothing important, it's just that I was doing something yesterday night and had completed it before going to sleep. But in the morning when I woke up, I see that the work is still undone. Just cannot remember when I had undone everything I had done in the night," explained Abhi.

"Are you sure you completed the job? Maybe you left it incomplete," enquired Aditi again.

"I am sure I completed it. I can't remember when I had undone it. This is what is intriguing me," said Abhi, frowning.

Aditi was amused at the success of the drug. So it was a sure thing that the victim would be extremely convinced that he had completed the job present in his mind last. It was better than what she had expected and felt sorry for her brother's confusion. But she knew the drug had no other side effect for a one time use and the experiment had been successful enough to be tried in a live scenario. She finished her breakfast and left the table, watching Abhi still grappling with his thoughts.

She needed to do some shopping, especially keeping in mind the next week's hectic schedule. It was this Sunday which she could use to buy some good dresses, perfumes and so on. She also needed some surgical gloves and of course some condoms and other pills to take care of any eventualities.

As Aditi left, Abhi also finished his breakfast, getting frustrated that he was late by one more day. Thank goodness it was a Sunday. But before getting back to his room, he wanted to take a walk around to the nearby park and soak in some sunlight to clear his mind. Abhi locked the door behind while coming out of his flat. He still had to find a way to intercept Uday Singh at the appropriate place and time. It should be a place and time where he could influence the event in his favour. He needed a chance to have some special me time with Uday Singh's laptop to enable him to insert his device as well as the bug. He would have to plan and then execute his meeting with Uday Singh in a manner to get enough time to infiltrate into his system. He would also have to restrict the time of infiltration to the minimum possible, may be a minute or so. He needed to practice the whole drill to gain expertise on completing the job with highest precision in a single chance that he was expected to get. While the lift dropped to the second floor, it stopped for another inhabitant of the building. Abhi greeted him with a nod of his head as he had met him once in a society function during Holi. He was carrying a laptop in his bare hands, without any bag, which reminded him of Uday Singh entering his car with his laptop in his hands, without any bag. This thought again made some of the grey cells move inside Abhi and he started thinking about his plans with this new realization.

Abhi came out of the lift and rushed towards the park with a renewed gush of adrenalin pumping in him. Along with clearing his mind, he now had to focus on the new idea coming to his mind. Once again, he needed to travel to the electronics market in the evening to give shape to his plans.

14th Day

The cool atmosphere inside the car was not enough to cool down Alka's emotions. She was very excited and wanted to have a full orgasm at this time of the day. It was in the morning while driving to office that she came across an exotic advertisement on a bill board, depicting the lustrous expressions of a half naked male model. She had suddenly felt a punch of excitement hitting her. Since then, she had been feeling highly erotic. As soon as she reached office, she checked if Rajal was in his cabin. Confirmed that Rajal had just arrived, she waited for an hour. Then she picked up a file randomly and rushed towards Rajal's cabin. After all the necessary protocol, she came face to face with Rajal. Being alone, breaking all barriers, she jumped on Rajal kissing him all over incessantly. Slowly she cooled down a little backing away from Rajal, who was looking at her shocked. Smiling Rajal asked, "Wow, what happened? Are you fine?"

"Oh yes, but I was thinking, we talked about having dinner together sometime, but can we have it today. And lunch instead somewhere in total seclusion, just you and me," replied Alka panting.

"Well, the condition you are in, I am looking forward to it now," winked Rajal.

"Okay let's move out by 1:00 p.m. today, and book your regular room for our special lunch," said Alka picking her file and rushing out of the cabin.

Since then, it had been very difficult for her to concentrate till Rajal gave her a call to come to the parking area. In the car, she turned the AC vent towards her to cool herself down, but it was useless with Rajal driving the car sitting beside her.

✦

Aditi went to the office pantry to have lunch with her colleagues. She was much more relaxed, having gained confidence over the possible success of her plans. She had successfully tempted Rajal, made a good deal and had tested another part of her plan successfully. Having a good laugh over petty jokes in the gathering made her forget the impending problems in her life. She thought over and over again on all the steps to be taken from that day itself. Running the whole script within her mind helped her to shed away the inhibitions of a novice. Imagining a situation repeatedly in the mind, putting oneself in the real life scenario helps a lot in preparing for the actual encounter. She just needed to hold on for some more time and it would be done and over with. Just a few more days, a little more manoeuvring and she would reach her destination.

✦

Biting her own lips, it was hard for Alka to cool down. As the car entered the hotel porch and stopped at the valet, she started trembling with excitement. Bubbling like a teenager, the mother of one was somehow capping her excitement as Rajal took the keys from the reception. Entering the lift, she had already pushed herself upon Rajal startling him. Rajal opened the room and let Alka in. As the door locked, Alka pounced on him pulling him, into her with full force and drowned her face into his curved chest. Alka pulled out his shirt out of the trousers and started unbuttoning him. Throwing away the shirt and pulling out the vest, she rubbed her lips and cheeks across the width of his bare chest. Rajal had also by then taken her hair out of all bondage. He pulled her to him with brute force and started pushing her towards the opposite wall. Basing her on the wall, he took off her sari and other clothes, draping her with equal speed and turned her to press her breasts against the wall, pushing his face into her back. With both hands cupping her breasts, he rubbed his lips from her neck towards her bare back down the spine. He then put a kiss and bit her on the hip which made Alka hiss loudly. Alka turned around pulling Rajal up clutching his hair, and then started pushing him towards the bed. As they reached near the bed, she pushed Rajal making him fall on his back on the soft foam with a thud. Alka jumped over him, sitting on top, with both legs stretched and then started her shower of kisses on Rajal, moving from his forehead, travelling down to his lips, chin, neck, chest, navel, thighs and back to the navel. Simultaneously, her hands kept caressing Rajal's body. Rajal had also been rubbing Alka's back and pulling her hair, getting aroused to burst any time.

Rajal started reaching his peak and in a fit to avoid wasting his fall, he got up and threw Alka on the bed, riding her and making the insertion in a controlled and smooth action. Placing his lips on hers and clutching her left breast, he travelled his right hand under her buttocks to hold the hip tightly. Thereafter Rajal started the eternal push and pull, under the ever increasing groans. Rajal was holding on to himself waiting for Alka to start her fall and released himself as soon as he felt Alka's groaning increasing and her vaginal walls squeezing him. He released himself with a loud groan, as loud as Alka's reaching the orgasm simultaneously. Completely spent, they both remained still for half a minute or so. Then Alka turned towards Rajal, pulling him into her embrace and hid herself in his chest again. Lying there in time which had lost its pace, they were left with a feeling of complete contentment.

✦

On the other side of the city, Abhi was not in a mood to work. His thoughts were still erratically drifting towards remembering the night before. Though he had reinstalled the device the day earlier, but still, he was grappling with the confusion and was annoyed having to invest his time again. Stealthily, he had been preparing the circuit diagram on his desk in the garb of doing office work on his system. He, however, could not focus on his system and abruptly returned back on the piece of paper on his desk where he was drawing the circuit diagram of another device which he had to prepare on priority. This device had to pack in a measured energy in a very small handy machine, not longer than a rupee coin. It had to be designed with a miniature circuitry and very tiny parts. Abhi was not very good at hardware but still much better than laymen in understanding the electronic circuits. Drawing the circuit diagram, he checked the complete circuit and then wrote the current and voltage readings along with size of the exterior attachment at the specified junctures on the diagram itself. Satisfied with his work, he folded the paper, kept it in his shirt's top pocket and got up to get some coffee.

✦

Abhi took an auto to the market to look for the components required by going from one shop to another. In an hour or so, he was able to satisfactorily collect all the required components. By the time he reached home, it was eight in the evening, but Aditi was not home yet. Abhi ordered pizzas again and placed all the components on the table.

He freshened up and shut himself in his room. Checking the feasibility of the circuit on paper and recalculating the voltage and current readings, he started placing the components serially in order of their getting attached as per the circuit diagram. Tucking the lens in one of his eyes, he then started designing the chip with the soldering machine and fixing the small components at the requisite places. Having affixed the circuit, he checked all the points with the multimeter and satisfied with the readings, he affixed the mini batteries in their place to charge up the device. As soon as he switched on the device, a single beep confirmed the activation of its functions. He then held up the device in his palm which was just one-fourth the size of a rupee coin. Black in colour, the device if affixed at the back of the laptop would not be easily visible. He brought it close to his laptop's base where the device self jumped and got stuck to the laptop. Abhi then opened the screen flap and switched the system on. The laptop screen blinked, but didn't start its boot sequence. The screen flashed again several times but nothing else, the laptop was not working. Abhi had a smile on his lips and then left the laptop on the table trying to switch it off and reopen it repeatedly, but it was of no use. For another fifteen minutes, the screen kept on blinking and flashing, but the laptop didn't start, and then the blinking stopped. Abhi lifted the laptop and detached his device from the base of the laptop. He put the device in the drawer and then again switched on the laptop. The system immediately started its boot sequence and the laptop became live with no signs of any malfunction. He appreciatively looked at his device lying in the drawer of the table. He took the device in his palm and changed the mini batteries with the new ones and kept it neatly in a small plastic bag, keeping it away safely again in the drawer. The temporary electromagnetic device was ready.

He then took out another set of components from the drawer and laid them on the desk, opening another circuit diagram. He then started off, without noticing the sound of the door opening and closing. This device was to work on the primary storage as well as the one which would connect with the programme he needed to introduce into the system and help the bug to perform its job unhindered. He continued for another couple of hours and after completing the job, remembered his empty stomach and the pizza cooling down on the dining table which he had received about three hours ago. He got up and went to the dining hall where one pizza box was still lying on the table while another was in the kitchen dustbin. He looked towards Aditi's darkened room and then sat on the dining table to finish his pizza. Having satisfied his hunger, returning to his room, he again checked both his devices, ensuring that he had not dismantled them again unknowingly. Having confirmed their safety, Abhi went to bed tired and content. Soon he was in deep slumber.

Aditi in the adjoining room, Rajal in a posh bungalow a few kilometres away and Alka also in a villa another few kilometres apart were deep in sleep. All three were actually dreaming something similar about each other. Similarly, all three were sleeping under the influence of alcohol. Sometimes in this world, we are not alone even in our thoughts. Aditi was dreaming of how she would manage her act with Rajal. Rajal was dreaming of how to snare Aditi and also keep Alka by his side. Alka was dreaming about Rajal. All three were standing on the same platform, looking in different directions, but hoping to board the same train.

15th Day

Raghubhai was nervous. Though he had been involved in all kinds of crime, kidnapping was not his forte. However tough he may appear, he also got intimidated every time he threatened any of his victims. Inside, he always feared that his victim may revolt against his own fear and stand in front of him challenging his mettle. The fear of ill happening is much bigger than the ill happening in reality. But now, on someone's instructions, he had issued stern warnings and threats to Abhi and tried to create fear by suggesting something he couldn't even think of. A threat should remain a threat only. If he had to forgo his threat or fulfil it, either way, he would be out of business. His business of fear was like his commodity trading – the trade runs till the time the commodity is actually bought by someone. His business of fear would also run till the time the fear remains and is not materialised.

Raghu had also been counting days and it had been fourteen days since he had issued the threat. If Abhi had not been able to arrange it till now, it would be difficult to do it in the six remaining days. Would that mean that he would have to resort to fulfilling his threat. Kidnapping a girl was the worst thing that he could think of. He worshipped several female deities and was not sure how he would handle this situation. He could not refuse Boss as he had been a godfather to him. No, he had no choice and was never given any choice, just a set of instructions to follow.

Having finished his pooja and back to his seat in the office, Raghu checked his opening balance and then looking at the pad on his desk, having latest prices of commodities he was interested in, diverted his focus to the trading world. A normal person does not choose to involve himself into antisocial activities; he just wants to live his life peacefully, without any conflict. But that is not possible sometimes; conflicts of life force him to tread on those paths which he never wanted to traverse through. Though there are some persons who get involved in antisocial activities just for the fun or the glamour of it, but they are those who cannot survive their consequences and get wilted before the fall. Raghu had to unwillingly set his foot on the path of becoming a ganglord to keep running his family business of money lending. He was not in a position to withdraw himself from this business now, as not only this was a more profitable business, but it also had a large amount of his money already circulated in the market which was not easy to extract at once. Even if he wanted to come out of it, the act was not possible as everyone in the market knew his financial position. Once he loses his fearsome gang lord image, he is most likely to become the victim of other gang lords in this field. In order to prevent himself from getting crushed under other fearsome peers, he had to keep up his own pressure of being equally powerful in this business. To keep his image updated, he had to now and then keep thrashing someone for some or the other reason.

Whatever he had done till now had been only symbolic, to generate a fear of possible harm he could inflict, but never a real harm to anyone. But this time he was nervous as he had been instructed to kidnap a girl. Though he had earlier extracted money from many wilful defaulters, this time he knew it was difficult. The time frame given and the amount involved was sure to make the inevitable happen. He even prayed that morning to God to help Abhi arrange twenty lakhs as soon as possible. At present Abhi's timely payment could save him from the criminal act he was instructed to do.

Raghu's dilemma was not only because of the kidnapping alone but the other heinous acts which he was asked to threaten Abhi with. He was very sure Abhi would not be able to meet the deadline and that he would have to act on his threat. The one idea which had been crossing his mind now and then was to refer the case to Boss again for extension of time. He had talked to the Boss the previous evening, but was strictly rebuked and was again instructed to do as told.

Since then Raghu had been toying with another idea; of helping Abhi covertly to arrange for the amount or he himself give him the required amount through some other means where neither Abhi nor Boss could get a hint of the help extended by him. After all, he had to save his own skin and twenty lakhs was not a large amount for sound sleep.

✦

The week had arrived; the week in which Aditi had the opportunity to make or break her future. She was a woman and as expected by this society, she had been looked upon as an object of desire only, to be utilised as an object. Why don't these men understand that the most important part of a woman's life is her sexuality which is her uniqueness and her personal disposition? If a woman's beauty and her physical features are attractive for others, that doesn't mean everyone is entitled to have his own personal piece of her space and time without her acquiescence. A woman's sexuality is always about her strength and it is her discretion whether to use her strength or not. Her sexuality is not a commodity, but a gift of nature.

Aditi had already decided that no one could exploit her body and that she refused to be seen or used as an object of desire only. She was one individual being, who had all the rights of a human being and hence is free to use her resources in any way she preferred. But why is always a man exploiting a woman by making her body the focal point? Why can't a woman do the same thing with a man's body?

This intense mental preponderance brought an idea to Aditi's mind. She could be involved in a sexual act with all the works with a man of her choice who already had plans of violating her and then blackmail him for her own use by using his fear of getting his heinous acts exposed in the domain where he could not afford to get exposed for this act. But then, it would be dangerous and also fraught with a lot of uncertainties. She would have to design a method by which she was able to exploit the opportunity without the victim knowing that he had been exploited. The present situation was one such opportunity where she could use her acumen to do the same. But in no way she could allow her body and soul to be violated forcefully.

Aditi had for most part of the day remained aloof from her colleagues. In the afternoon she called Rajal and confirmed her meeting for the evening. It was a five star hotel in the midst of the city. She always wanted to have a look at this hotel from inside, but never thought it would witness an important but secret event of her life. After noting down the room number which would be the arena for the day, she fixed an appointment with her parlour for the evening. Thereafter she again tried to rehearse her part for the evening.

During lunch, Abhi went out for some time to the nearby market where he had seen a small toy in the toy shop. This was a small ring which had a hidden instrument used to pinch another person by making the outer portion touch another person's skin and pressing a little lever at the back of the ring. He checked and tested it by wearing on his finger and pinching his other hand. It worked perfectly. He had all the tools now and just had to implement each stage of his plan as per the blueprint in his mind. There was no other backup plan, so he had to be accurate at every step. Back at office, he made some frantic efforts to complete one more part of his project, but then left it getting frustrated. His personal task was more important. As the time was nearing for the actual performance, he had butterflies in his stomach. At one point, he felt nervous enough to think of backing out, but then thinking of Raghubhai's threat, got courage to go ahead with his plan.

Coming out of the parlour, Aditi felt refreshed and looked forward to the evening which seemed was going to be an exciting one. She took a taxi to hurry home as she needed to be ready by the time Rajal came to pick her up. Reaching home, Aditi went straight to her wardrobe to take out the red sari she had got dry-cleaned a month earlier. These occasions called for red and pink; colours which were known to increase the licentious hunger of men. Dressing herself in red would help her make Rajal go mad about her. After she had finished dressing up and had finished putting on her make-up, she looked at herself in the mirror and gave her image an appreciative flying kiss. Being confident, she went to the kitchen to have a glass of water to cool her anxiety. She sat on her bed taking deep breaths and trying to rehearse in her mind how she would handle the situation.

It was 7:00 p.m. when Aditi's mobile rang; it was Rajal. Aditi took a quick look at herself in the mirror swinging sideways and went out to meet him. Rajal was standing beside his car when he saw Aditi coming towards him. She looked stunningly beautiful, making Rajal pat himself in his mind for clinching a perfect deal. As Aditi came close and greeted Rajal, he opened the door and gestured to Aditi to enter. When Aditi made herself comfortable, Rajal smiled looking into her eyes and closed the door softly. He got in and turned the ignition on and before putting the vehicle in first gear, extended his hand towards Aditi. She reciprocated smilingly by extending her hand and putting it into Rajal's. Rajal took her hand up and kissed it gently, then slowly took his hand towards the gear knob to shift the gear.

Reaching the hotel, Rajal and Aditi went straight to the pre-booked room, the keys of which were already in Rajal's pocket. Aditi tried to cover her face, looking down to hurriedly enter the lift and then crossing the lobby to enter the room. Once they were in the room, Aditi relaxed, while Rajal was feeling quite at home. Closing the door and locking it from inside, Rajal held Aditi in his embrace and moved his face closer to Aditi's. As he was just over her lips, Aditi turned away and started to wriggle out of Rajal's hold. Feeling her discomfort, Rajal released her from his embrace and gestured towards Aditi with his wide open extended hands.

"I am feeling a bit uncomfortable, you see it's my first time and I don't know how to handle it. Give me some more time," said Aditi in a trembling voice.

"Oh sure, that's fine. We have all the time in the world. Let's have something first, what would you like to have? Tea, coffee or some soft drink?" said Rajal, comforting her.

Aditi looked at him and in a hushed voice said, "Can we have something stronger? If you don't mind, I think I need to have some more courage."

"What will you have, beer or scotch? We have some here in the room bar itself."

"Let's have some scotch," replied Aditi.

Rajal took out a scotch bottle and prepared two standard pegs with ice and soda and took them to the centre table where Aditi was already sitting. Both lifted their glasses and toasted to themselves and started drinking. They began chatting about work and so on.

While Rajal emptied his third peg, Aditi was still not halfway down her first. Rajal understood her inhibitions over her slow drinking by the facial expression she made with every sip. He knew the taste would seem horrible for those who had never tasted alcohol earlier. To ease her down further, Rajal put on some romantic music on his iPad and while finishing his third, asked Aditi for a dance. Aditi agreed and held Rajal's hand to get up. Rajal again put his arm around her and placed the other hand of Aditi on his shoulder. They both started gyrating to the tune and slowly started pushing themselves into each other. Aditi clung on to Rajal, keeping her head stationed on Rajal's chest and kept grooving with him for some time. Rajal started kissing on her head, taking in the enchanting smell of her glossy hair and then slowly moved his lips to her neck, rubbing them up her ear. He held her head back, and tightening his embrace, he put his lips on Aditi's, pressing them hard. Aditi also let Rajal enter her mouth and started enjoying the tingling, letting the excitement overpower her. Slowly, Rajal started unwinding her sari and then opening the zip of her blouse, slid it down her arms. Holding both her bare breasts in his palms, he started pressing her back towards the bed. Here, Aditi again stopped him, and then slowly unbuttoned Rajal's shirt and took off his vest. Aditi then asked Rajal to lie down on the bed while she went to prepare one more peg. Rajal took off his trousers and slipped into the bed while Aditi went to the table and made another drink, finishing it in one single shot. Rajal lying on his bed was watching Aditi's bare back with her shining hair flowing up to her waist. He was staring at Aditi and was still trying to make himself believe that after such a long wait, Aditi, his fascination, was standing half naked just few steps away from him. That in the next few minutes, she'd be lying beside him in his bed, completely naked. Aditi took the glasses and turned towards the bed, climbing on it, sat cross over Rajal's thighs and handed him his glass. Both again started having their drinks and while Rajal finished his drink, Aditi put her glass on the side table after taking two sips and lay down on Rajal, kissing him on his chest and neck. Rajal also kept his glass on the side table after finishing his drink and started caressing Aditi's back. Rajal was still in awe and trying to believe that finally he had Aditi in his embrace, the one whom he had been desiring for the last two years.

✦

Some kilometres away, Abhi closeted in his room with his cold pizza was running tests on all the devices he had made. They would decide his success or failure. With so little time left, he had to check everything that day itself. There was no time to change or carry out any major improvisation. Now he had to stick with his preset plan and there was no option for his machines to malfunction at this point of time. The next day, he was expected to receive the storage chip which he had ordered online. Every other component was ready and live. He had made a slot to insert the incoming chip for data storage. But he could still check all the features of the devices. He opened the laptop he had brought today from one of his friends with the excuse of improving its processing speed. He checked the software and other features of the system and ran some programmes to improve the overall processing speed. His friend, whose laptop he had brought, was of non-technical background and used the system mainly for surfing and gaming. He used to take the help of Abhi whenever he encountered any issues with his system. Abhi then switched off the laptop and turning it upside down, opened the back cover, exposing its motherboard. He checked certain connections and then plugged in one of his devices to one of the open ports, attaching the device at an open space with a double sided tape and then placing back the cover, screwed it tightly.

Abhi switched on the laptop again and when the boot sequence completed its regular cycle showing the detection of a new device and installation, he immediately plugged in his data connection. Simultaneously, he booted his own laptop and connected his mobile phone's internet through wifi. Both laptops were now connected to the internet through different service providers. He then ran the software he had developed on his own laptop, which after sometime routing itself through the long world of internet showed a connection established and produced a different screen in a window smaller than the desktop. Abhi looked at the screen on his laptop and the screen of the adjoining laptop. They were identical. He then opened some files on his friend's laptop and made some notes on office software. Then opening the mail box he mailed that document to one of his other mail boxes. Coming back to his own laptop, he opened one of the folders on the duplicate screen where he could see the same mail and its attachment. In other folder on his laptop's hard disk, he could find the mail and attachment stored in a specific chronological way. All that he did on his friend's system got recorded in a folder on his own laptop which when run with another of his software showed exactly the same steps he had done on the other laptop. Satisfied with the results, he then disconnected both the laptops and switched them off. He then opened the back cover of his friend's laptop again and detached the device. Keeping both the devices in his bag, he went to bed switching off the lights. Then suddenly got up to go check Aditi's room. The pizza was still lying packed on the dining table. He put it in the refrigerator and wondered why Aditi was still not home. It was 12:30 a.m. He went back to his bed and was soon fast asleep.

A few kilometres away in the hotel room, Aditi was sitting on the sofa near the window, looking out at the bright sky above and the empty road below, puffing out the smoke from her lungs. She turned her gaze inside to drop the ash in the ash tray and glanced at Rajal lying naked on the bed, lost in deep sleep with a satisfying smile on his face. Aditi smiled and then turned towards the window, placing the cigarette back on her lips, relaxing her mind inhaling some poison. She was feeling a little exhausted, but not sleepy. She had many thoughts running through her mind and was thinking about the coming few days when she would have paid the amount, bringing an end to the nightmare.

16ᵗʰ Day

The light drizzle was making the sun rise up shyly. The breeze was moist. The light earthen smell of the soaked earth entering through the nostrils scintillated the body and the mind, making them yearn for more rest. Abhi had a long day ahead. It had become more of a do or die situation. Thinking about the pending work, he began cursing the same weather which was making him poetic a few seconds ago. He got up and toiled to get ready for the day. He had requested the package to be delivered at his office address.

Getting up rubbing his eyes, Rajal saw Aditi lying beside him with her bare back towards his side. He placed a light kiss on her back and leaving her sleeping, went to the washroom. On the other side, Aditi smiled at hearing the washroom door close and suddenly jumped out of the bed to cover herself up and sat on the sofa, waiting for Rajal to come out and show him her guilt. A few minutes later, when Rajal came out, he saw Aditi sitting on the sofa with her face towards the window. Rajal came up to her and extended his hands to run through her hair, but she shoved them away and that was when Rajal noticed Aditi's moist eyes. He sat beside her and asked, "What's worrying you?"

Aditi kept looking towards the window silently, without answering. Rajal pushed himself closer and embracing her from the back, again questioned, "Can I help? Something related to me?"

Aditi burst into tears and turned her face and hid it in Rajal's chest, embracing him tightly. "I don't know, yesterday night I broke away from everything. My honour, my chastity, my identity, my uniqueness, my purity, my pride – I lost everything. A momentary passion and I have lost my life forever, now nothing remains the same," she murmured weeping.

"Oh come on, what nonsense? This does not change anything. You are still the same as before, and instead of losing everything, you learned something new," consoled Rajal. But Aditi kept weeping, holding Rajal tightly in her embrace. Rajal also held her and kept caressing her hair.

After some time Aditi calmed down and slowly separating herself from Rajal said, "I think we must make a move, it's getting late."

She stood up and went to the washroom. In the washroom, Aditi wiped her tears, smiled at her image in the mirror and kept staring at herself for a few more seconds. She needed to tread carefully; her aim was to get the required booty as early as possible without damaging her own self.

Meanwhile Rajal got ready and ordered some breakfast. He sat on the sofa pondering on why Aditi was crying and he understood it was the first time for Aditi, but he was struggling to remember her expressions the previous night. Had she been terrified? Did she try to stop him? But he didn't remember, it was a beautiful exotic night and he felt good about it. Then why was Aditi upset? Was losing her virginity such a big deal? He couldn't understand, but he was forced to think about it again. The breakfast arrived and was served on the table. After a few minutes, Aditi also came out looking stunningly beautiful without any artificial touch-up. They both had their breakfast in silence and got up to leave the room. "So I will pick you in the evening at the same place?" asked Rajal picking his blazer.

"Well, I will call you. I don't know about today evening; give me some time to think."

Rajal was taken aback. "Why, what happened? I think everything was great."

"Yeah, but give me some time. I need to think," said Aditi.

"But now how does it matter, now that we have spent time together, it should not be a concern anymore," Rajal continued.

"I understand, but please ... I will call you, just drop me home now. I need some time alone," said Aditi while coming out of the door.

All the way to Aditi's building, both remained silent, lost in their individual thoughts and enjoying their individual victories. Reaching the apartment building, Aditi got out of the car and said, "Before coming to pick me up, wait for my call."

"Fine, I will wait for your call. But once again I want to say, there is nothing to disturb your mind. There is nothing wrong that we did; we only enjoyed our togetherness, so just take it easy. Well ... Good day," Rajal bid her goodbye and drove away.

Aditi kept watching Rajal's car going out of her sight, then moved towards the lift lobby of her building. Reaching her apartment, she realised that Abhi had already left for office. This is what she wanted. She had already taken a week's leave from her job. Aditi freshened up and smiled several times. Thinking about the night, she went to bed. She had no time to waste and needed to get prepared for another rendezvous.

Abhi had reached office early and was waiting in the sun to warm himself. In order to avoid getting noticed by his colleagues, he went across the street and stood behind a cigarette shop. His eyes were on the entrance of his own office building and were continuously watching every car arriving in the building. After waiting for approximately fifteen minutes, he could see Uday Singh's car slowing down and turning towards the entrance of the building. Abhi crossed the street and went inside the building following the car to the basement parking and waited beside the lift looking towards Uday Singh's car as it stopped for a few seconds for Uday Singh to get down and then the driver took it away to park it at the designated place. Uday Singh was holding the laptop in his hand and came to wait outside the lift along with six or seven other people; some of them greeted Uday Singh. Abhi also greeted him and stood behind him, maintaining a distance of two men between Uday Singh and himself. As the lift came down and the doors opened, Abhi slipped in, standing at the back while Uday Singh also entered the lift and stood among all the others. Uday Singh had to go to the seventh floor, while Abhi's office was on the sixth floor. Uday Singh got out at the seventh floor while Abhi went up to eighth floor and coming out of the lift, rushed down two floors to reach his office. Abhi had noted down all the points which were important and tried not to miss any detail. Coming back to his desk, he made a flowchart to present all the activities he had noted in pictorial form to enable him to refine his plan further.

Abhi had noticed close circuit cameras at the entrance and in parking area, covering each of the entry and exits in each block of the parking. In case of anything going wrong, he had to have an alibi. Thinking for some minutes he then called one of his friends and asked him to lend him his car for one day. He needed to be able to justify his presence in the basement parking on the day of his venture. He had noticed the way Uday Singh clutched his laptop and identified spots where he was required to focus. Abhi then called the courier agency whose number he had taken from its tracking site. Talking to the courier, he demanded the urgent delivery of his packet since this delivery was a key component for his plan and his plan could not take off without the delivery of the storage device. Abhi relaxed upon hearing that his packet was out for delivery and would be delivered to him in the next two hours. Abhi then went on to focus on his official job.

He, however, just kept fiddling with his system while waiting for the delivery of the storage device. It was presently the last piece of the hardware he required to start his operation. He was waiting for the delivery but somewhere remotely his mind did not want it to happen till infinite time. Once it got delivered, he would have to take the final plunge which would end in either success or failure.

◆

Having sex had always been an exotic, exciting and fulfilling experience for Rajal, but he was confused why the previous night's escapade with Aditi had not been that fulfilling. It felt like there was something missing and he was not able to feel enriched as he had been feeling when he received anything much desired by him. Rajal was not able to come to terms with the fact that he had fulfilled his long standing desire but was still not feeling satiated. He felt like he was too hungry, had eaten the most delicious recipe and his stomach had become full, but he neither remembered the taste nor did he feel wonderful about it. An uneasy feeling was prevailing over him. Everything seemed distasteful.

It seemed that his experience with Alka had been much better and exciting than the one with Aditi. But why was it that he remembered every move and every act with Alka, while he could not recollect his time spent with Aditi, except some faded memory of having sex with her. It may be that when we long for something too, much then suddenly getting it fulfils the whole journey of longing and thus brings an end to the craving. Sometimes the end of the journey is more painful than the journey itself. The period of the journey is full of expectation and wait for the destination, but when we reach the destination, the related expectation and wait comes to an end, thus finishing the very purpose of the journey. Then suddenly a vacuum gets created and it gives rise to this type of melancholy.

Rajal guessed that the same thing had happened with him also. Over the last couple of years, he had wanted to have Aditi in his embrace and have a full blooded sexual engagement with her. His planning and effort over these years to achieve his desire had occupied him so much that now when he had achieved it, it had not felt that exciting.

Rajal got up from his bed and made a drink for himself. He had skipped office and was in no mood to talk to anyone. Lying down, sipping his drink, he remembered having too many drinks the previous night too. Though he never drank too much to lose his senses, he still felt it had affected him way too much. Rajal decided not to have drinks that evening and enjoy his night to the fullest. But then he remembered Aditi weeping and doubted that she'd spend the evening with him. Once again, the wait was starting to give rise to the same desire.

Aditi had said she would call if she was able to gather enough courage. But Rajal was getting impatient; he had never felt such longing earlier with any of his sexual companions. It was different with her; his desire for her had been with great intensity. Over the period of the last two years, he had several times dreamt of playing with her, having sex and enjoying every part of her. But when he had actually experienced it in reality, he did not feel satisfied and it still felt like he had enjoyed it only in a dream.

At around 2 p.m., his phone rang. He picked up the call. He heard Aditi's husky voice apologising for her behaviour and then asked him to pick her up at the same time, and the same place. Rajal felt a rush of blood and instantly rejuvenated as he disconnected the call. He lay down again and started pondering about what had gone wrong the last evening. He could only deduce that he must have done the act in a highly inebriated state. This could have been the only reason why he could not feel the satisfaction. He decided not to have any alcohol and devour the pleasantries in his full senses that evening.

◆

Abhi received the package and simply kept it in his backpack without trying to check the item. He didn't want anyone to notice that he was in possession of any device of this sort. He finished his work as early as possible and rushed home to complete his main device. After reaching home, he immediately unpacked the small chip and fixed it inside the main device he had built. Attaching the device to his laptop, he first checked its working without inserting the batteries and then he again checked it with its battery cells on. In both conditions, the device was working fine. Abhi once again laid out all the devices on the table in front of him and revising the whole plan in his mind, he ran his fingers over all his creations once more, feeling proud of his skills.

◆

Alka had finished her day's work and was free. She found that Rajal had not come to office. She then called on his cell phone which went unanswered. Being free, she was thinking naughty thoughts and wanted to spend some time with Rajal; that would be better use of her free time rather than surfing on the net or reading something new. She had never been an academic sort and had just studied enough to get a decent job. Luckily, she had enough brains to know how an opportunity is grabbed and used to its best result. Also, she was aware of her physical attractiveness and was very well conscious about her special features which instantly attracted the opposite sex. Even after a successful pregnancy, she had been able to maintain her figure perfectly. Most of the things being male oriented in this world had helped her understand what men want. Alka always took it upon herself to deal with men in a manner which suited to her needs. She always took strong decisions and used this shortcoming of men, to think themselves superior to women, for her own use. She never let herself be mowed down by men and lived life on her own conditions. When she married Padam, it was her own choice looking at his physical attributes, his social standing, his earning capacity, his nature to match with her requirement and of course his ability to handle her freedom.

Alka and Padam had been a very unique couple, who believed in maintaining their separate identities while living together as a couple. They also made sacrifices for each other, not under the compulsion of their bondage, but because of the responsibility towards each other and their family. With their separate strengths and weaknesses, they always supported each other in each other's times of emotional crisis. They were friends married to each other without having a feeling of possessiveness for each other. They were after all human beings and not things to be possessed. The most contentious issue with most of the couples is their partner's relationship with individuals of opposite sex. This issue was openly discussed and agreed upon with each other. They both gave freedom to each other in having relations with the other sex, but also promised to remain committed to each other. And it was very clear with them that commitment to each other did not necessarily mean having sex with each other only. They could remain committed to each other even if they enjoyed sexual relations with others. They were a detached couple with individual identities. Over these years they had been able to experience more happiness than any other couple, having spent time together in a live-in relationship. They never had to quarrel on anything as they had already extinguished all the reasons because of which couples usually fight. As far as sex was concerned, they always supported each other by having sex together with each other or letting the other satisfy himself or herself with someone else of their choice. They never made this a highly personal and sensitive matter in their relationship. They loved each other, detaching themselves from each other; they didn't become each other's part, but were complete with each other. Their relationship seemed to be more spiritually inclined where bodies didn't matter, but souls did. It was not a bonding but bondage of freedom, a commitment towards each other's liberty.

Summarising her day's work, Alka once again checked if there was anything which needed to be attended by her. Having found nothing which required her attention, she decided to call Padam. She planned to meet Padam in an hour at the coffee shop in between both of their offices and on the way to their home. She lifted her purse, instructing her secretary while coming out of her cabin and left for the parking arena. She reached the coffee shop and finding her favourite table available, grabbed it, waiting for Padam to arrive before placing the order.

✦

Aditi got up at around 4 p.m. after having a long nap and then took a warm bath to freshen herself up. By 6 p.m. she was again completely ready, emitting a heady fragrance from every corner of her body. In a light yellow suit, she made a French braid tying her hair neatly. She gave herself the look of an Indian homely girl blushing at simple conversation. She wanted to finish her expedition with Rajal that evening, but knew how difficult that would be. She knew it was not going to be easy to end it all prematurely but the insecurity of giving herself up was looming large. She was afraid of being caught. She called up Rajal and asked him if he could do a favour by bringing the deal amount with him as she needed it immediately. Rajal expressed his inability as it was too late for a withdrawal from the bank. Aditi impressed upon the urgency of her request to which Rajal agreed to provide it first thing in the morning. Aditi agreed feeling victorious and waited for him to pick her up.

✦

Alka and Padam sat in silence, just looking outside the window, sipping their coffee. They didn't need to talk to each other in words to understand each other's needs. Both felt relaxed just having coffee with each other.

"So your boss is doing fine?" asked Padam.

"Yes, he has his own world. Did not come to office today," replied Alka. Then again after a silence of few seconds she asked, "You have any plans for tonight?"

"No, nothing. I will be home, do you?"

"Nothing, that's why I asked if we can be together?"

Padam smiled and pressing Alka's hand on the table said, "That's what I wanted to ask you as well."

"Well then, I suppose we should finish our coffee and rush home, we have a son waiting for us," said Alka.

"Didn't you enquire why Rajal didn't come today? Has your charm worn off?" asked Padam sipping his coffee.

"No, I know where he is. He is trying to fulfil one of his long standing desires and once it is done, he will come back to me. I don't allow my prey to escape my clutches till I want it to," said Alka laughing.

"So he has designs on someone else also?"

"Nope, I met one of my sister's old classmate a few days back in a bar. She confided in me about her deal with Rajal as she was in urgent need of some money," replied Alka.

"So that bastard now takes advantage of another person's helplessness," said Padam angrily.

"That's what she was also worried about, so I helped her."

"But how could you help her, did you expose him or what …"

"No, I just gave her the ideas which would help her fulfil Rajal's desires and simultaneously relieve her of the pain of having to succumb to Rajal."

"Oh great, I believe you. What's the name of the girl, do I know her?"

"Yes, you've met her once … Aditi … we met last year at a party."

"Hmm … I can't recall her … but forget it, so what about today? Is he with her ?"

"May be or maybe not, but his absence has something to do with her. Okay, now forget it; she has handled him earlier as well and I'm sure will do so now. Let'go home, today I have some evil designs on you," said Alka as she got up holding Padam's hand. Padam held her by her waist and paying for the coffee, came out of the cafe. They headed towards their individual cars in a hurry to reach home.

✦

Settling down in the hotel room, Rajal preferred having coffee in the room itself with Aditi. He was not in a hurry and wanted to enjoy the moments in his complete senses. Holding his cup of coffee, he pulled Aditi to sit beside him on the bed, while he himself stretched his legs. Aditi also sat comfortably and started sipping her coffee looking at Rajal. She could clearly see the lust in his eyes, but was not scared.

"Are you comfortable now? You seemed quite disturbed in the morning," asked Rajal.

"A bit nervous again. I don't know how to handle this. I actually wanted to spend time with you, but not in these circumstances."

"Then in what circumstances, now don't tell me that you wanted to marry me?" ridiculed Rajal.

"No, may be not that way, but since the day we met, you had created a special place. If it was not for your proposal that night, maybe we could have had a different relationship," said Aditi.

"Well, we could still have had that relation but you distanced yourself from me and I hesitated to approach you again because of the guilt from that day," said Rajal, thinking he had always been right about his mistake of approaching her too early that day.

"I had distanced myself not only from you, but had in a way distanced myself from most of the male influences and that was all because of my experience with you," explained Aditi.

"Then why did you contact me again after so many years?"

"Well, I expected you to accept my deal in view of your exceptional interest in me," smiled Aditi while explaining her point. "And I needed this money urgently."

"What is such urgency for such a large amount that you are ready to compromise with your own values?" asked Rajal.

"I can't tell you this, it is extremely personal," said Aditi finishing her coffee.

"But now you seem to be rethinking your decision. First you got me to cancel our outstation trip and then your behaviour in the morning ... that's why I ask you if you are comfortable," said Rajal.

"Frankly speaking, I am not and I want to end it here itself. The society from where I have come and where I have grown up, we have been taught several rules informally, one of which is to have this type of relationship only after wedlock," said Aditi. "I know you find it strange that we had discussed about spending one week together, but now it seems that I need more time to prepare myself," Aditi kept on saying, while taking off her clothes piece by piece. "Though I am asking for some more time to prepare myself mentally, I am in dire need of this money."

"Well that is not an issue, if you promise me to be able to spare time for me in future, when you have reconciled with yourself, we can have a continuing relationship," said Rajal.

"Yes, that would be so," said Aditi while slipping into bed beside Rajal.

"Fine then take your time, I will wait," said Rajal while embracing her tightly in his arms.

Aditi remained in his embrace for a few minutes, then wriggled out and said, "Can we eat something first? I am feeling hungry," Rajal agreed as he was rather hungry too.

The order was placed and then both dressed up again to wait for dinner to be served. Rajal went to the washroom while Aditi served both of them. They finished dinner watching television, just like an average Indian married couple. Aditi finished first and washing her hands, she asked Rajal if he wanted a drink, which Rajal refused unwillingly. But Aditi prepared two glasses, keeping one in front of Rajal and holding one herself. She sat in front of Rajal, sipping from her own glass. Rajal wanted to gulp down both the glasses at once, but he controlled himself. By the time Rajal finished his dinner, he had unknowingly emptied the glass kept in front of him and then regretted breaching his promise to self. When he came back from the washroom, he prepared one more drink for himself and passed it down his throat. Realising that he was again having a drink, he sat down to gauge his consciousness level. He felt balanced and gaining confidence that he was not drunk, he got up and held his hand towards Aditi. Holding his hand, Aditi also got up from the couch and coming closer, pushed Rajal towards the bed, making him lie down. Taking off her clothes, she sat cross legged over Rajal's thighs and bent her face on his chest. Rajal held her in his embrace, bringing both his arms to her back and tried opening the hook of her bra. After some struggle, he was successful; taking a long breath, he started pulling out the bra. Aditi also felt her bra strap loosening up and waited for a few seconds for Rajal to remove it, but then she felt Rajal's hands slowing down. When his hands became stationary, she lifted her face to see Rajal taking short breaths in his deep slumber. Smiling, Aditi got up, tightened her bra again and put on her shirt. She went to the table, prepared a drink and moved towards the window, taking the glass with her. Pulling a chair towards the window, she sat on it stretching her legs against the window pane. Aditi then looked outside the window, sipping her drink slowly.

In another half hour or so, Aditi finished her drink and then resting for another half hour tracking the headlights below on the street, she got up to close the window and return to the bed. She first stood behind Rajal's head and pulled him up by holding him from his shoulders. She then unbuttoned his shirt and took his vest off. Thereafter she pulled off his trousers and briefs. She looked at the naked Rajal sleeping in front of her, and smiled at her work again, just like she had the previous night. She had mixed the drug in Rajal's drink the previous day, but had mixed few drops in his dinner that evening. The drug was working wonders.

Rajal lying naked in front of her was tempting Aditi to take the plunge, but she controlled her desires and determined herself to stick to her original plan. In no way did she want to jeopardise her efforts at this moment to make the whole exercise worthless. She took out the surgical gloves from her purse, and climbing over the bed, sat with her legs spread across over Rajal's knees. She caressed both his thighs, and sliding her palms slowly upward, she grasped his penis between her palms. It was already tightened with Rajal dreaming deep down of having the foreplay with her. Smiling, she started massaging his extended limb, forcing more blood to pump in. Having him completely drenched in excitement, she made him eject all his desire in another few seconds. Aditi had got highly excited during the whole activity and was having a tough time controlling her own libido. As she finished with Rajal, she rushed towards the washroom to clean herself up. In another few minutes, she cooled down herself with a quick bath and came back into the room, making herself another drink.

Having finished her drink, she looked at the watch. It was already two and Rajal would not be up before six, so Aditi decided to go back to the bed and have a sound nap. She got up and moved towards the bed, picking up Rajal's briefs. She put his briefs on again, and turned him on his right, while she herself lay in the same bed on his left, putting one of his hands on her waist. Intoxicated with alcohol and her success, she fell into a deep sleep very soon. Another day would begin in a few hours, another struggle will surface in a few hours, hope will emerge in just a few hours.

17th Day

A bhi was quite restless and could not concentrate on his *pranayam*. As the sun rose from the horizon and the darkness started to give way to the fresh grey morning, Abhi was just a few hours away from collision. He needed all the courage to go for the kill in the single shot. He would not get the chance of any retake for this once in a lifetime shot. Again and again, he tried hard to throw out all his thoughts, but somehow the same thoughts pushed themselves into his mind. The repeated efforts at last weakened away his nervousness and let courage sneak in a bit. The *pranayam* helped him a lot to grasp his own being and think about his major target, take care of his priority and advance towards completion of the job in hand. Gathering his devices, he went to get ready for the day ahead.

Abhi was out of his building and on the street in the next half an hour. Taking an auto, he went to his friend's house, whose car he was borrowing for the day. While in the auto, he had lost track of all the other movements and traffic around him. He was only visualising the event he had to make happen, repeatedly in his mind. For him the event could happen only once and if anything went wrong, there was neither remorse nor correction. It had to be correct in the first and the only attempt. Whatever practice or rehearsal required, he had to do it in his mind. Every stop at the red light relieved him a lot because of the delay it was causing towards the actual event time. He had several times thought of backing out, but fate had brought him to a juncture in life where he had to plunge into acts of debauchery. He again had a thought of informing Uday Singh about the fraud he was going to commit, expecting he would help him out by offering the amount he required, but then had to desist from it since it was a risk he could not afford at this time.

Lost in his thoughts, he heard the auto driver informing him of reaching the destination. He looked out, surprised at reaching the place so soon. He got out and paid for the auto. Crossing the street, he entered the building housing his friend's flat. In another fifteen minutes, he was driving a small car towards his office.

It took him twenty more minutes to reach his office. Stopping nearly twenty metres away from the main gate of his office building and looking out across the street at the entrance gate, he began perspiring. He had not felt this nervous even when he had come for the interview of the job in this building. Taking out some items from his folder, he transferred them to his jacket pocket. His fingers were twiddling with the items in his jacket pocket while keeping an eye on the main gate. One of his devices in the form of a ring was already encircling his ring finger. The ring had a small button towards the palm side which could be pressed from the thumb easily. This was a readymade prank device he had bought from the market, but had altered it a bit in its output power, increasing it by some more volts. The other devices were in his pocket, which were to be used later in the day. His eyes were fixed on the gate and the road passing through it scanning every person and vehicle entering the gate.

As time elapsed, Abhi became more nervous at the thought of Uday Singh not coming to work. Then his eyes noticed a black Mercedes approaching the gates. Abhi immediately recognised it, started the ignition and moved ahead to be able to precede the Mercedes. He moved ahead fast to be able to park his vehicle in the parking even before Uday Singh's car could enter it. Rushing towards the lift lobby, he noticed Uday Singh's car slowing down. Abhi's heart started thumping hard seeing Uday Singh carrying his laptop in his hands as usual. Abhi then paced himself to remain just behind Uday Singh and stopped behind him in the lift lobby. As the lift came down and opened, he entered the lift along with Uday Singh, making sure to stay right behind him, which was facilitated by several other persons entering the lift.

As the door closed and the buttons were pushed for the requisite floors, Abhi took out his hand from the pocket holding one of the devices in his palm. He wiped the sweat from his forehead and then had a good look at all the other persons in the lift, most of whom were looking up at the panel indicating the floor numbers. The lift was to stop at the third floor first and he had time only till the sixth floor. He had to act then. Abhi took his hand close to Uday's and brushed it slowly and casually, to which there was no reaction from him. He then took his hand close to Uday Singh's hand holding the laptop and looking at the display panel of the lift, put his thumb on the button of the ring in his finger. As the lift stopped at the third floor and its gates opened, simultaneously Abhi pressed his thumb.

Uday Singh hissed, "Ouch."

He dropped his laptop on the floor and looked at the back of his hand surprised at what had happened, while Abhi knelt down to pick up the laptop. Abhi straightened up with Uday's laptop in both hands and asked,

"Any problem sir, the laptop slipped from your hand."

"Ah nothing. I felt a little sensation in my hand and the laptop slipped. Thanks, I hope it is not damaged," said Uday.

"Don't worry sir. Even if it is damaged, you can call me. I am on the sixth floor, name is Abhishek and extension number – 4263. I will check it and fix it," said Abhi while holding the laptop and discreetly attaching one of his miniature devices to the back of the laptop. After caressing his hand, Uday took his laptop again and thanked Abhi.

As the lift stopped at the sixth floor, Abhi while moving out turned to Uday Singh and said, "Remember extension 4263, Abhishek, if there's any problem with your laptop," waving smilingly, he went out. Uday also acknowledged him as the doors shut.

Abhi came to his workstation and switched on his system. He was feeling ecstatic at the way it had gone. He had visualised all this happening several times in his mind and had tried to find solutions to every obstacle he may have had to face in the event of anything going wrong. Abhi relaxed on his chair, gulping nearly half a bottle of water placed on his table. Comforting himself, he logged in to his system and started checking his mailbox.

Abhi looked at his landline and picked up the earpiece to check the dial tone. He then again shifted his sight to the monitor, leaned back on his chair and waited.

The phone suddenly rang; he waited for two rings and then picked it up, "Hello, Abhi ... I mean Abhishek here."

"Ah Abhi, how is your progress on the C section?" It was Jacob – his partner on the same project.

"Oh, Jacob, just hang up. I am expecting an urgent call," said Abhi annoyingly.

"Oh boy, is some gal going to call you?" chirped Jacob.

"Just hang up and don't disturb me," Abhi said and disconnected.

Abhi suddenly got tensed. He should have called by now. It was his only chance. What if Uday Singh had called some other engineer from his floor itself. Abhi could not think; it was becoming difficult for him to concentrate on anything. Every other second he looked at the phone and then calculated some more seconds. Every second seemed like a year to him. Half an hour passed. Uday Singh must have resolved the issue or may have got another engineer by now. Or it was possible the device had not worked and everything was fine with his laptop. For another five minutes Abhi just sat on his desk with his left hand palm on his forehead, feeling defeated. Losing hope, he got up to get himself some coffee. He was five steps away from his table when he heard the phone ring. Turning towards his desk, he looked at the phone. Was it Jacob again or ... Abhi ran back to his seat and picked up the hand piece, "Hello, this is Abhishek."

"Hi Abhishek, this is Uday. Can you please come to my cabin on the seventh floor?"

"Aaa ... Yes sir, I am coming right now. Is there any problem with the laptop?" Abhi asked sheepishly.

"Yes, I think some internal damage because of the fall, can you just check? I remembered you telling me your number," said Uday.

"Sure sir, coming in a minute," said Abhi. His heart was again thumping fast against his rib cage and he was ecstatic to be back in business. He checked the second device in his pocket, took the portable tool box and then rushed towards the lift.

On the seventh floor, he moved towards the enclosure where Uday's secretary sat. "Hi Reena! Uday sir is expecting me," said Abhi.

"Yes sure he is expecting you, please go in fast," said Reena directing him towards the cabin door.

Abhi knocked twice and opened the door slightly, "May I, sir?"

"Yes, come in. I think the fall has taken its toll. See if you can fix it," gestured Uday, turning the laptop towards Abhi.

Abhi sat on the visitor chair, pulling the laptop towards him and tried to switch it on. Waiting a while and seeing no response from the machine, he turned it upside down and pulled out a screwdriver from his pocket. He detached the battery and then unscrewing the back cover, exposed the main hard disk and motherboard parts. He started an animated checking for the different wire connections, the soldering points and other such points. He pulled out the RAM and then re-fixed it securely. Abhi was doing everything very slowly and cautiously, not to disturb any other setting of the hardware. Uday looked at Abhi's working for some time and then got up from his chair, "Well, I think you will take some time to detect the issue. In the meantime, I have to make some calls," saying that, Uday went on to sit on the sofa at the other end of the room.

Uday's back was facing Abhi, so he could now work without fear. After taking stock of Uday's position from the corner of his eyes, Abhi slowly pulled out his device from the pocket and instantly fixed it inside the laptop, attaching it to the already open port. He then fixed the device securely on the surface with the already gummed side of his device, and detaching the first device which he had attached at the back in the lift, and pocketed it secretly. Abhi then placed back the back cover and screwed it back. Turning the laptop over, he switched it on and immediately connected his pen drive in its USB slot. As the system started its boot sequence, it detected the pen drive and the pen drive started its job. The software was designed in such a way that with the help of the device connected by Abhi, the system would override requirement of administrator login for the installation of the malware. The system booted completely and halted at the login screen. Abhi pulled out his pen drive assured of the complete transfer of the malware, and then called Uday.

"Sir, I think the problem is sorted out. Can you check by logging in if everything is fine now?" said Abhi.

Uday got up and turning the laptop towards him, he punched in his login details and waited for the system to log him in.

He then checked some of its functions by opening some of the files and his mailbox. "I think it's working fine. What was the issue?" asked Uday.

"Nothing sir, I think the RAM got loose during the fall and was not connecting to the socket," said Abhi casually. "I will leave now, if you have some other problem, just give me a call, I will check it."

"Oh thanks, I will … thanks again. You saved me a lot of hassle," said Uday, shaking hands with Abhi.

Abhi then left the cabin and ran down to his floor without waiting for the lift, as if he was trying to flee a crime scene. He immediately gulped down the other half of his bottle of water as soon as he reached his seat. He then took a deep breath of relaxation. The job was done.

✦

Rajal was still not sure why he was not able to feel the ecstasy and enjoyment of the time spent with Aditi. He felt better with Alka, though he had never desired her so badly. But with Aditi, he felt something was missing and was not able to figure out what it was. It seems he needed a break from Aditi, may be that would help. Rajal kept pondering over it for some time and then tried to shift his focus towards his job. He engrossed himself in his system for another few hours, keeping the Aditi factor out of his focus. After two hours that morning, his phone rang with Abhi's name flashing on the screen. He suddenly remembered the job he had given to Abhi and the importance of this job occupied his mind, completely pushing aside other concerns.

"Ah Abhi, where were you? Heard nothing from you all this while. Are you still working on it?" enquired Rajal.

"Oh yes, of course. I have been working on that and it is nearly done. Are you prepared with one system of yours with a high speed data connection fixed?" said Abhi.

"Yes, I got it installed in my office," replied Rajal.

"Okay then, I'm sending a software file and a batch file on your mail ID. Just install that software on your system and then run the batch file. I will come in late today to explain the other details," said Abhi.

"Fine. I will wait for your mail. By what time will you be coming?"

"By when is the office empty?"

"You can come by 8:00 p.m. There will be no one. The guard will show you to my office," answered Rajal.

"Okay, I don't want any employee of yours to see me meeting you. Being from a rival company, it will be difficult for me to explain my presence in your office," said Abhi.

"Well then I will wait. Hope you have done it well. And be assured I will take care of my part of the deal. Bye," said Rajal disconnecting the call.

Rajal pushed himself back on the chair with both his hands at the back of his head and turned his thoughts towards what he had been planning to achieve from all this exercise. If Abhi had been successful in his venture, then Rajal would hit a long shot in his business. Rajal, coming forward, bending on his laptop, flipped through the files on his system where he had prepared the costing for the new project he had to bid for. He fine-tuned some costs and marked some areas with red colour to be checked afterwards, once he was able to use the programme Abhi had made for him. His bid for the project was to be finalised and submitted the next week. He had enough time, but before that, he had to check what his rival companies were planning to exhibit. His quotation had to be better than them and less in cost terms for the user company. The project was big enough to launch his company into the big league of software solutions, which would bring him long term stability and international visibility. He was ready to pay any price for this project and was even ready to have a predatory pricing in his bid.

Having completed the review of her projects, Alka ordered a coffee and stretched back on her chair. While she switched her focus away from her computer screen, it instantly drifted towards thinking about Rajal being away from her for some time. She hadn't been able to meet him the past few days. Whenever she enquired about him, either he was not in office, or he was busy as her secretary always told her. Was he avoiding her or was it really a busy time for him? Was her grip on him loosening? She knew Rajal was preparing for an important project, but then, she also had some plans for him. She had risked all she had to get through to Rajal. But still, Rajal was keeping her at an arm's length. He only spent some time with her, but never made her privy to his other plans. She had been a project head for a long time and it had reached a point of stagnation. She needed bigger projects and a larger exposure, which could be provided by Rajal through his latest venture. She had taken all these efforts to ensure that when Rajal searches for a project head for his new project, then her name should be foremost in his mind. She needed a prominent position enough to launch her in the international scene and that could be done only through Rajal's next project. Finishing her coffee, Alka dialled Rajal's secretary once again to seek an appointment. She was immediately confirmed for a meeting. Alka felt relieved and checked her notes diary to review her points, which she had prepared to pitch. Then she got up and moved towards Rajal's cabin to have a fruitful meeting.

✦

Less than a week was left and Aditi was still not sure whether she would be able to arrange such a large sum or not. Every passing day, Aditi feared that she might get caught by Rajal. That would be a disaster for her. She would not only lose everything she had been doing, but the threat she had feared may materialise. Whatever was to happen, it would be quite clear in the near future. Somehow, she had to end it; lingering on would not only elongate the uncertainty, but also the fear of failure. Aditi got up to go to the washroom to freshen herself up as she had been taking classes continuously for the past five hours. She had cancelled her leaves and joined the institute. She had to think of a way out to wind up her rendezvous with Rajal. She had to be perfect in her plan to end it since what ends well is a job perfectly done.

Aditi wound up her work and bid goodbye to her colleagues. It was still daylight outside. She suddenly noticed a man outside sitting in front of the tea shop at the opposite side of the road. While she was still on the first floor of the stairs hidden behind the tinted stair wall glasses, that man was watching the main exit gate of this building. She had noticed the man in the last few days, hovering around. She noticed him since he looked familiar, as if she had met him before. Was he stalking her? If so, where else had she seen him? Aditi stood at the stairs looking outside, focussing on trying to remember. Concealed behind the tinted glasses, she took a good look at the man and stressing on her grey cells, she remembered having seen him on a bike behind her as she alighted from an auto on reaching home. He had been standing under a street light while she was boarding Rajal's car, had been sitting on the footpath bench outside her building and now was at the tea stall outside her office.

She became sure that the man was following her and had some devious intentions. She again stressed on her mind to reminisce how she seemed to know him from even earlier than his recent spotting. Then it came back to her. She trembled as she remembered he was the man she saw from her room's keyhole being the most vocal along with Raghubhai, and if she remembers correctly, his name was Bholu. Oh my God, had they already assumed that Abhi would not be able to arrange for the demand and hence they had already planned to abduct her on the due date? Was it a part of their pre-planning or had they made up their mind to violate her in any condition? Aditi started sweating on thinking of the possibilities linked to the man who had been stalking her for the last few days. She had no choice but to stick to her plan and then finish it the way she wanted and certainly not in the way these people wanted. Aditi gathered some courage and then started moving downstairs to exit from the gate and watch Bholu. Now when she was aware of the presence of a stalker, it would be easier to handle the situation. But this also made her shed all her inhibitions about her adventure with Rajal. She now felt a stronger urge to deal with Rajal and achieve her objective. She started pacing towards a parked auto rickshaw and glancing by the nook of her eye, she saw Bholu also kick-starting his bike.

Abhi, reaching the office of Pranam Enterprises headed straight towards the eleventh floor. He did not have to ask for directions or get any access permission to Rajal's office, since he already had the magnetic access card provided by Rajal to facilitate unhindered entry into his office. Rajal was sitting on the sofa, waiting for Abhi. As Abhi entered closing the door behind him, Rajal signalled towards the desktop installed on the left side of his side table. Abhi went straight to Rajal's chair; without exchanging any pleasantries, turning towards the desktop, he checked its configuration and the connectivity speed. Satisfied, he took out a pen drive and connected to the system's USB port.

"Sir, the whole setup will take some time, you can rest for the time being. Can you please order a coffee for me? I need it badly," said Abhi.

"Well, all the sub-staff have already left. Just wait, I will get you a coffee in ten minutes," saying that, Rajal went out of his cabin.

Rajal took approximately fifteen minutes to get two cups of coffee while Abhi remained engrossed in downloading the software and then making his own settings to enable the programme to run smoothly with all its attachments. It took him around half an hour to get the system configured as per his requirement. Checking everything again, he gestured to Rajal to come and have a look. Abhi stood up and offered Rajal his chair. Thereafter, he started tutoring Rajal about different functions of the software.

"You are now connected to Uday Singh's laptop and whatever he does on his system will get transferred to you through the internet cloud and you will have his screen mirrored on your desktop," explained Abhi.

"Will I have to man my desktop the whole day in anticipation of expected data?" enquired Rajal.

"No, it is not required. Everything will get recorded on your system's memory itself and you can access the same as and when you feel like. It will be like a storehouse of all that Uday Singh will do on his system," Abhi further explained.

"Okay, so the data will keep on transferring and getting stored. It will be easier, thanks, I think that should work fine for me," said Rajal.

"Yes, that will give a complete read access to whatever he is doing and I hope that would fulfil your requirement," said Abhi.

"Hmm ... that should, am impressed. But you said it is cloud based; that means it is hosted on some server which is also storing this information?" said Rajal.

"Yes, but that is temporary. The software in your system will delete all the data from the cloud once it is downloaded on your system, while the other storage is inside Uday Singh's system itself and is secure. It also stores data temporarily till it gets enough connectivity to transmit it to your system," explained Abhi.

"Fine. It seems perfect."

"I will leave now ... and if you think I have done my part of the job, then should we finish with your part too?" said Abhi, though fearing it was too early to demand his payment.

"Yes of course. Meet me tomorrow at the same joint where we had coffee and we will settle our business," replied Rajal smiling.

Abhi took his bag and turned towards the door to rush home. He would have to wait till the next day to get his dues and also relieve himself of mental pressure. It had been the focus of his life for the last few days. Once this is over he would return back to his regular life, thought Abhi as he came out of the office building and waved at an auto-rickshaw.

Rajal took a good look at the desktop again and then pulled himself back on his chair, pulling in a deep breath to calm down his mind. His thoughts wandered towards the upcoming project where he needed all help from this desktop to pull in some hard data matching his bid for the project. Rajal checked the time; it was 9:30 p.m. and time to pick Aditi for another night with her. Strangely, Rajal didn't felt excited about the whole affair of spending the night with Aditi. It seemed more like a burden rather than ecstasy. He felt astonished at his own feelings and thought of putting an end to the arrangement. He had made up his mind and in the morning itself had withdrawn twenty lakhs from his account, stashing it in the glove compartment of his car. Pocketing the keys of his car, Rajal exited from his cabin to hurry towards the parking lot, feeling much more energetic going to end his bash with Aditi.

Aditi was quite sure she would be able to finish off her deal with Rajal as she waited for him outside the coffee shop. It was strange that Rajal planned to pick her so late, and instead of meeting at their usual place at the bus stop near her apartment, he planned to meet at the coffee shop. She was wearing a sleeveless suit which made her feel the chill. She wanted to go inside and have a hot cup of coffee, but had to wait outside as Rajal was to just pick her up and then move on to the hotel. She checked her purse again, she had stacked the drug inside the hollow of one of her empty lipstick cases. She had to hide it carefully, fearing if Rajal ever smelled foul play, he may check her person. As time ticked, her anxiety levels kept increasing; why was it that Rajal had decided to meet so late. Must be work; after all, there are other important things in life, pleasure is not always a priority. The chill along with a light breeze reignited the urge for a hot cup of coffee and as Aditi turned her face towards the coffee shop, she could sense Rajal's car turning towards her.

Rajal brought the car to a halt and got out of it just as Aditi was about to walk to the passenger's side.

"Come on, let's have some coffee! It's quite chilly."

Startled, Aditi felt relaxed since she needed that cup badly before embarking on her adventure. They went inside and sat at a corner table. Aditi felt loosened up from the stiffness of the cold outside, but was rather astonished at Rajal's calmness. He also looked quite relaxed and seemed to be in no rush, as against his usual eagerness. Even though they were starting so late, Rajal seemed to have all the time in the world. He ordered two cappuccinos and then tapping the table with his fingers, roved his eyes across the cafe. It seemed Rajal was trying to avoid eye contact with Aditi. Once the coffee was served, they picked up their cups and started sipping it quietly. Halfway down the cup, Aditi said, "I really needed that!"

"Yes, it is a cold day ..." acknowledged Rajal.

"It seems your day has been too busy and tiring," said Aditi.

"Not really, it's just that it seems what you expect does not always happen the way you want and I usually don't like things happening out of nowhere. I like to remain in control of everything, so when events don't turn out the way I wanted them to, it makes me fret," explained Rajal.

"But every time, thing don't happen as you wish, it certainly does not make them wrong or unsatisfying. We should enjoy the unforeseen," said Aditi.

Rajal looked at her and said with a smile, "You may be right but if things don't happen your way and it doesn't seem to excite you, then it is better to forget it and carry on with life to search for another avenue which will make you feel more satisfied."

Aditi kept sipping her coffee, trying to gauge the conversation and how it was related to her or the present arrangement between her and Rajal. Was Rajal referring to their present sojourn and had become suspicious of what Aditi had been up to? Or had he honesly not been able to understand what had been going on between them? Whatever it was, Aditi was listening with her heart in her mouth.

"Well Aditi, I think the arrangement between us has worked out quite well, and in my view we have enjoyed it to the fullest possible. At least I had, and am sure you also share the same feeling," said Rajal without looking at Aditi.

"Yes of course, I did enjoy myself," said Aditi but then added hurriedly, "But you know, my purpose was different and hence I am focussed towards my goal."

"Yeah, I understand. I think since we have other engagements in life and our focus is towards different goals, we must move ahead. What do you say?" said Rajal.

"In my view, though we have different engagements but this arrangement of ours is also one of them and we should take it to completion. I am willing to complete my part as I have a lot at stake," said Aditi fearing Rajal may terminate the arrangement prematurely.

"I think you fear that I will not keep my word," Rajal said as if hearing clearly the words of fear emanating from Aditi. He added, "Don't worry, we will part on a happy note. Let's go now; it's already past ten."

Opening the passenger door of the car, Rajal made way for Aditi to settle down. He came around to take the driver's seat and then drove towards the main road. Aditi wondered what he had planned next. It had been an ordeal for her, and more so, it was not going smoothly at all. She was now preparing herself to let the things go as they should go. She decided she would not use the drug that night and would let Rajal take his bite in reality. She had to compromise because if Rajal backed, she had a more ruthless future ahead. The way that villainous character had been following her had already given her a hint of what awaited her if this plan failed, and she was terrified.

As the car stopped, Aditi realised that they had reached their destination and as she looked at Rajal, she wondered whether he was staring at her lustrously or was it compassion? Did he know her situation? Aditi took her eyes away from Rajal and was surprised to see that they were in front of her apartment. What was Rajal up to?

"Don't you think we are in the wrong area? That's my house!" exclaimed Aditi.

"Yes, I know it's your house. I think it was a nice experience with you and I will remember it for life, but for now I think we should bring it to an end," said Rajal, looking into the astonished eyes of Aditi.

"An end! Means? But I need the funds now, my requirements cannot wait any further. Try to understand, it's just not possible ..." Aditi became hysterical.

"Hold on, hold on ... didn't I tell you that I will complete my part? I will not end it here without fulfilling my part," saying that, Rajal extended his left arm towards the backseat and picking a packet brought it in front, placed it on Aditi's lap.

"Here, my part. Twenty lakhs as agreed by us in the beginning," said Rajal. Aditi astonishingly touched the packet on her lap and then turning towards Rajal said, "But we still have some more days to go together ..."

"I know, but that's all for now. I think it's too late and you should move now, we will remain in touch," saying so, Rajal caressed her cheeks and moving closer, pulled Aditi's face towards his, holding her hair lightly. He slowly joined her simmering, nervous lips with those of his. Aditi also brought her hands to hold Rajal and gave her complete self to the parting kiss. They finally parted from each other's embrace, getting back to their seats, trying to suppress their ignited feelings.

Rajal got out and came around towards the passenger door. Opening the door, he held it for Aditi to alight from the car. Aditi alighted slowly, clutching the packet tightly.

"Well thanks for completing your part, I really needed it," said Aditi coming out of the car. Rajal wished her a good night and kept looking at Aditi while she entered the main gate of her apartment building.

While driving back, Rajal felt quite relaxed as if he had been relieved of a heavy burden. The mental relief now made him think more clearly and his thoughts quickly drifted towards the job just completed by Abhi. He intended to make complete use of it; the project had to be bagged by him at all costs. The way things had turned out in the last few days had given him a lot of satisfaction. Everything was shaping up in the fashion he had planned, except the Aditi episode, which had left him a little bitter. But he knew he would be able to overcome it with the huge success he is expecting from his other venture. Rajal was so sure of bagging the project that he had started planning for its execution too. But proper execution required a leader who could take it forward in the right way. Out of all his leadership staff, his mind kept drifting towards Alka, as she had recently been closer to him than the others. Alka had all those qualities which were required in a leader of a project of this scale. Since this project was to occupy most of his time, it would also mean more time with Alka. Now that the Aditi episode was over, Rajal began to feel ecstatic thinking about Alka again. The future seemed to be clearer with many pieces of life falling in line.

✦

Entering the lobby, Aditi turned back to check whether Rajal was still there, but there was no sign of him. She looked down at the packet she was holding, still not believing that she had achieved her goal, and without having to compromise. Had it been so easy or just pure luck? Aditi entered the lift and being alone, rested her body against the wall after pressing the button. She was anxious to tear open the packet and count the amount down to the last note. The lift seemed to be moving too slow and as each floor passed, the tingling in her fingers kept increasing. Her achievement had still not sunk in. As the lift door reopened at her floor, she jumped out and running into her flat, headed straight towards her room. Locking her door she immediately tore open the packet and there it was: ten bound bundle of notes of fresh two thousand denomination. She put them down on her bed and kept staring at them in awe. She then flipped through them to ensure that all the packets had notes of five hundred rupees only. Then she stuck her nose into the notes to take the smell of the notes down her nostrils. She had never seen such an amount at a go and was more awestruck realising that this was all hers now. She was still trying to believe that her destiny had favoured her so much … that she could achieve her goal in such a short time. It was a miraculous event in her life, for which she now not only kept thanking the almighty, but also swearing in His name not to repeat this kind of sport in future. Though it had been rewarding this time, but the imminent risks in this type of projects are too grave to be given a second chance. It was a once in a lifetime opportunity which she got and her courage had taken her through it. Aditi gradually fell asleep over the notes, realising that her ordeal had come to an end and. The morning the next day would be much brighter and full of hope for a new day.

Abhi heard her sister come and go straight to her room and locking it immediately. He wanted to go and ask about what had happened to her, but he was in no mood of spoiling his own disposition. He needed no interference in his private space where he wanted to enjoy his success by himself. The next morning would bring an end to whatever troubles and tribulations he had been undergoing. There was no sleep in his eyes; he was just sitting on his bed counting every second left for the new day to begin. The day which would witness in all its splendour the unfolding of the new era of his life where he could achieve anything he wanted to, if he wanted to.

✦

Rajal parked the car and went straight to his floor; he got his cabin opened by the surprised guard. Asking the guard to bring him coffee, he settled down on his chair and switched on the screen of the desktop besides him. The screen came live and as he clicked the relevant icons, the guard brought him his coffee. By the time the links opened and the guard left the cabin, he took two quick sips. Turning back to the screen, the smile on his lips started widening up and the lines on his brows started straightening. It seemed he had a lot of work to do now and take things to completion by turning the events in his favour. He took the coffee cup and giving a sideways jerk to his head, kept staring at the activities being displayed on the screen. "Uday Singh does a lot of work himself, it seems. Good," murmured Rajal.

"Good for me ... well done, Abhi, you deserve applause ..."

18th Day

The dawn was bidding the darkness of the night goodbye. Aditi was still in her deep slumber with note packets littered all across her bed. In the adjoining room, Abhi was still half asleep and half awake watching the wall with his drowsy eyes. His wait for daybreak seemed to be lengthening as the wall across was slowly coming into vision with day light seeping through the window behind him. He couldn't wait to call Rajal and fix a meeting. The venue had already been decided, but the time had to be fixed. Abhi was feeling quite sleepy, but the uncertainty in his mind was not allowing his mind to rest. After all, it was a technological solution, and that also created in a short time without too much of scenario testing. It may fail in some circumstances which he may not have envisaged. He knew Rajal would first completely test all his requirements on the system before making a payment. Since Rajal was himself a technocrat, he may himself detect some issue which may make the whole solution a waste and worthless for his needs. There were several such questions and situations running through his mind. He was just praying to God to keep the system working at least till the time he received his payment.

Finally a ray of sunlight could drill a hole through the clouds and passing through the window behind Abhi made its mark on the wall. The announcement of the new day instantly ran a life current inside Abhi and he jumped up to get fresh to welcome the day with an invigorated mind and body.

As Aditi's eyelids started making way for the daylight to seep through her retina, it started messaging the brain to get up. Finally, getting up on her feet, she stretched and looked at the watch, it was past 9:45 a.m. It was too late, but she was in no hurry. Picking her phone, she messaged her manager saying she wasn't well. Aditi sat beside the window to look outside and smiled at the irony of her message. She had never felt better than this and still had to take leave for not being well. With a long yawn she got up, gathered all the packets scattered across her bed, counting them to be ten in number and stacked them below her bed mattress. She then came out of her room to make some coffee for herself. Abhi's room was already deserted. He must have reached his office. Was he also trying to arrange this amount or was he relaxed and doing nothing? This thought had crossed her mind several times during the last few days, but then she shrugged it off as she knew her brother must be trying hard to deal with the problem. Aditi wondered whether she should have talked to Abhi before embarking on her mission to arrange for the amount herself. May be he had already arranged it by some means and the pain taken by her may have been in vain. Whatever it be, it was now time to talk to him.

By ten, Abhi had become impatient, having played with his pen for over ten minutes now and gulping over two cups of coffee. He couldn't focus on his job. Though he had come to office early, it was not because of his work but to vent out his anxiety. He had to get hold of his well-earned money and waited for the time to pass so that he could call Rajal. He needed to make the call and keep his hopes alive for the day.

Rajal woke up hearing his phone ring and rubbing his eyes checked his watch. It was 10 a.m. the phone was flashing the name of Abhi.

"Yes, good morning Abhi, tell me ..."

"Good morning. I called you to confirm at what time are we meeting today? We had fixed the venue but didn't decide the time, so I thought I should call," said Abhi a little hesitatingly

"Oh yes, let's meet at 1:00 p.m. Is that okay?" said Rajal calculating mentally the time he would need to go back home, freshen up and reach the coffee shop as decided.

"That will be fine, see you," said Abhi enthusiastically and hung up.

Rajal got up, and checking the desktop to see if everything was fine, decided to head home. He needed to freshen up and then wind up his business with Abhi for the time being. But he also understood the need for maintaining his relationship with Abhi for any future assignment. As Rajal came out of his cabin, he saw Alka walking towards him.

"Hi, Good morning, you look so shabby, have you been here the whole night?" asked Alka.

"Ah yes, it was something important. Couldn't wait till the morning, anything important?" asked Rajal.

"Yeah, wanted to talk, but not that important ... you can take your time," said Alka.

"Well then, I have a meeting this afternoon. We can meet for late lunch at three at our regular venue," said Rajal with a naughty smile.

Alka replied, "Sure, we can talk during lunch. It would be a better environ to discuss what I have to say," Alka also wanted to talk during those tender moments when it would be difficult for Rajal to respond unfavourably.

"Well then, I will pick you up, see you," said Rajal walking towards the lift.

"Sure, see ya ..." said Alka turning back to take the stairs for one floor down to her office.

Finishing his pending work by 12:30 p.m., Abhi took leave of two hours from his project leader and went out towards the street shop where he had to meet Rajal. Abhi walked to the meeting place which was just about two kilometres from his office. Walking fast, he reached the shop in twenty minutes. As he was just looking around, he saw Rajal's car coming towards him. He was bang on time. Few minutes later, Abhi and Rajal were sipping coffee in paper cups sitting inside Rajal's car as Rajal told Abhi happily about how the system was working well and he had been able to extract some very useful information from it. Abhi was relieved. As they finished their coffee, Rajal brought out a packet from the rear seat and handed it to Abhi, "Here, twenty lakhs in cash. You've earned it."

✦

Alka had just finished her last assignment when she got a call from Rajal to meet him across the street in ten minutes. In another half an hour, Alka felt comforted in the hotel room kissing Rajal passionately after so many days. As they fell on the bed, Rajal seemed very excited to have all of her in a single bite.

After enjoying the delectable, sumptuous lunch, Alka once again dragged Rajal back to the bed. As she started caressing his chest, Rajal took her face in her palms and said, "I don't know, but you give me immense pleasure. This should have happened much earlier."

"Hmm … I also find you much more compatible than my hubby Padam. We should have met earlier," smiled Alka rubbing Rajal's lips with her thumb.

"For the last few days, I had been engrossed in some project and hence had not been able to give you time, but today you drenched me in your charm. You are marvellous and adept in making love. I fear I may fall for you," said Rajal carefully choosing his words.

"But I think … I have completely fallen for you," said Alka while climbing over Rajal, holding his head from the back and kissing him.

For the next few minutes they forgot everything else. As they slowly separated their lips, Alka fell down on Rajal's chest with closed eyes. Cooling down, Rajal brushed his fingers through Alka's hair and said, "My God, you are magnificent, I think if you keep going like this, I will get ready for another round in the next fifteen minutes."

Alka kept quiet, lying on his chest, slowly rubbing Rajal's arm. Alka asked, "So what has been keeping you busy all these days? Was it that important …".

"Well, you know, I have been trying to get this project which will catapult our company into the largest line-up, I have been busy planning for that," explained Rajal.

"Then if this project is that important for you, then let me handle it, baby. That way you can have both, the project and these heavenly escapades of ours," said Alka, playing her cards well and at the right time.

"Yes, I do agree with you," said Rajal.

"So tell me when should I start and from where …" said Alka.

"Well we will start, but for now, I think I am prepared for another round, let's not waste time," so saying, Rajal turned Alka around climbing over her.

◆

Abhi returned to his office, checked his backpack again while keeping it inside the bottom drawer of his desk. The packets were lying safe in the backpack. Abhi was again not able to concentrate on his job, as now he wanted to rush out of the office and take out those packets to count the money. He couldn't believe he had been able to solve the problem in such a short time. It was a miraculous effort which had also given him a lot of confidence about his skills. When he thought back at what he had done, he realised that he had discovered a new method in the world of espionage and data leakage. He started realising the value if he carried on these activities as a profession where he could help companies to steal data of other companies with such ease. Abhi then tried to clear his head of the thoughts and concentrate on his work.

By the time Rajal returned to office, it was nearly empty. Alka went straight to pick her car, while Rajal took the lift to his office floor. Sitting in his chair Rajal again switched on the desktop screen and started checking on the stored files. He could already feel the chill down his spine checking the available files. Though these files were not what he wanted, still it was fun checking what his adversary had been doing. He ran some searches to find the relevant documents related to the project he was interested in. Searching by all possible ways for more than an hour did not give him the required details. Tired, finally he switched off the screen, deciding to check it again the next day. There was no question of the system not working as he could see many confidential documents of Uday Singh during the search initiated by him. Abhi's system was working but then whatever systems Abhi had used, there must be something implanted very near to Uday Singh, which was in synchronisation with Uday's laptop, and was capturing and transmitting every activity being done on the system. Rajal would have to wait for the moment when Uday prepared his quotation statement and stored it on his laptop, which would be the defining event that will be the actual product delivery from Abhi.

It was nine in the evening when Abhi reached home. He had lost track of time as he was finally able to work on his project with a free mind. Returning to normal life was much of a relief for him after the maddening fortnight. As Abhi entered the flat, he saw Aditi on the sofa watching television.

"So you are back, isn't it quite early by your standards?" chirped Aditi. She seemed to be in a good mood. He also realised that he was meeting his sister after a long time. Abhi kept his bag on the other side of the sofa, sat beside Aditi and said, "Yes, I guess I was able to finish early today but you have also not been home at your regular time these days, didn't you go to the institute today?"

"I didn't; just wanted to rest. What will you have, tea, coffee or dinner?" asked Aditi.

"Let's have dinner first. I'm so hungry," said Abhi.

"I just ordered it, you go and change. I will lay the table," said Aditi.

It had been a long time since both of them had sat down together for dinner. They were both relaxed like students who had just completed their exams. While eating, they chatted about random things. Finishing dinner, both sat down on the sofa to watch television. As Abhi was changing channels, Aditi looked at him and noticed that Abhi looked quite carefree. May be Abhi had somehow got his time extended or had arranged for some money. But whatever it be, she had to now confront the situation.

"So how have you been doing these last two weeks?" asked Aditi.

"Quite fine, nothing special … just regular days," replied Abhi casually.

"Nothing special … even after having been threatened by Raghubhai?" queried Aditi.

"What! Raghu who …" said Abhi startled.

"The one who threatened you because of the money you owe him."

"How do you know I owe money to Raghubhai?"

"Well, I heard him barking at you that day and threatening you with certain consequences," said Aditi.

"You heard him that night?"

"Yes … I heard it from my room."

"Oh, so you know the threat …"said Abhi adding, "but you don't worry. I will manage it. After all, was just a threat."

"You will manage? How? The amount is huge and time short. and I know all your resources are already exhausted. When were you planning to tell me all this? After they'd have hurt me?" said Aditi turning aggressive.

"No … But there was nothing to tell you. I had been working on it and that's why I didn't involve you …" explained Abhi.

"That's not right. At least I could have run away, if that was possible. I must have had some alternative," said Aditi. She added, "When an event relates to a human being and specially your sister, you ought to tell her and seek her help."

Abhi listened with his head tilted back and then said, "Okay, sorry. I understand that, but I think you are blowing it all out of proportion."

"Am I? Tell me … then I ask you … or I should say I demand you give me five lakh rupees now … let me have it … give me!" said Aditi turning towards Abhi extending her right palm towards him.

"Hey take it easy, it is not easy to arrange five lakhs instantly. I don't have it," said Abhi.

"If you don't have it now, then tell me when will you give it to me?" pressed Aditi.

"Well, I need time … give me a few months, I will arrange it," said Abhi lightly.

"That's it, I knew it … if you need few months for five lakhs then you will need few years for twenty lakhs. How do you think you were going to arrange it in twenty days? Do you think I am dumb?" saying so, Aditi got up and thumping her foot on the floor, paced towards her room. Abhi was astonished and kept looking at her. Before he could assert himself and answer back, he saw Aditi returning with something in her hands.

"Here, take it …" said Aditi putting the bundles of two thousand rupee notes on the edge of the table in front of Abhi.

Taken aback, Abhi exclaimed, "What's this?"

"Twenty lakhs … just pay off Raghu and throw him out of our lives. I got it arranged … just make him vanish from my thoughts," said Aditi holding her head between her palm.

"But how did you arrange for it in such short time?" said Abhi, picking up one of the bundles and looking at it carefully.

"First things first …just pay off and end it," said Aditi.

Abhi picked another bundle as well! It was not a small amount. He had been toiling a lot mentally to earn it and here it was in his hands, just given to him effortlessly. He could do a lot with the twenty lakhs. Many of his aspirations could be fulfilled and he could again try his luck in the stock market, from where all this had begun. Holding both bundles, he wondered from where had Aditi got all it. She must have taken a large loan which will be difficult for her to repay.

"Have you taken a loan from somewhere?" questioned Abhi.

"Who will give me a loan for this huge an amount. I am a salaried person and you know my salary," replied Aditi.

"If you have taken a loan, then tell me ... it's not a good idea to repay one loan by taking another. It just creates a vicious circular trap where there is no escape," reiterated Abhi.

"Come on, I have not taken any loan. This is my money, which I arranged myself and I don't have to repay it ... you can use it to repay the loan and get us out of this mess," said Aditi.

"Are you sure you don't have to return it to anyone?" asked Abhi reconfirming.

"Yes sure, no returning ... this money belongs to me," replied Aditi.

Abhi once again looked at both bundles in his hands; he weighed them, felt them, smelt them, then shrugged his head to ward off some unwanted thoughts and kept both bundles on the table, pushing it towards Aditi.

"Well thanks a lot, but now I need only ten lakhs. I have also been able to arrange for ten lakhs and was tensed to find ways for arranging another ten lakhs. You just saved the day," said Abhi looking at the bundles on the table, not able to match eyes with Aditi.

Aditi looked at him surprised and gestured, "How did you arrange ten lakhs in such a short time ... and were you hopeful of arranging the rest in the next few days?" questioned Aditi.

"No, I have ten with me and with your ten I will repay the loan and get rid of the likes of Raghu," assured Abhi.

"Well then that's good, just fulfil your promise," said Aditi pulling five of the bundles on the table towards her. "But are you sure you have the other ten or are you still arranging it?"

Abhi went to his room. Returning in a few seconds, he had five bundles of two thousand rupee notes in his hands. Keeping it beside the first five bundles, he said, "Now it's twenty, happy? The figure is complete."

Abhi looked at Aditi, then looking back at the bundles on his sofa, smiled again. "So now we can claim our life back again and forget it all as if it was a bad dream."

"You are smiling! Do you realise that with just a few days left, you were only able to arrange half of it, what would have happened if I had not arranged for the rest?" said Aditi apprehensively.

"I was planning to give half and then buy some more time from them," said Abhi looking down, trying to hide the guilt in him. His conscience was pricking him to come clean with the truth, but greed was heavier than the guilt.

"And what made you sure that you would be given extra time?" gestured Aditi.

"Nothing, just a hope that the deal will be struck," said Abhi casually.

"Hope! Did you ever apply your mind, do you understand the consequences or did you ever think of what would have happened with me ... or ...wait a minute ... did you even listen properly to what they had said about me?" shouted Aditi, standing up in rage.

Abhi didn't reply and looked at the bundles on the sofa.

"Are you listening to what I am saying? God damn I am your sister, didn't you think about what would have happened to me?" said Aditi raising her voice on seeing Abhi watching the bundles. "What are you looking at so intensely?" said Aditi again, irritated.

"Sshh," gestured Abhi putting his index finger on his lips. "The bundles you brought and the bundles I have brought have been banded with same bank's note-slips and the date stamps on them denote the same day, which means both the bundles have been withdrawn from the same bank, same day," explained Abhi. Aditi came nearer and bending over both the bundles watched the note slips. Then she checked the note slip on the bundles in her hands; it also bore the same note slips.

"What if along with the same bank and day, they have been withdrawn from the same account?" exclaimed Aditi.

Looking at each other they both said simultaneously, "Rajal!"

19th Day

Raghu was still not up when his phone rang. Rubbing his eyes and grappling in the dark, he tried to read the caller's name. Comprehending the caller's name, he jumped out of his bed with his eyes bright open and instantly picking up the call said, "Yes Boss, so early? Everything fine?"

"Yes everything fine, just ask your man to stop following Aditi. My interest in her whereabouts is over now," saying that, Boss hung up.

Raghu just listened and wondered if this was such an important instruction that the Boss had to wake him up in the middle of the night. He checked the watch; it was five in the morning, but still dark in the room. Raghu went to the window and pulled the curtains. Standing by the window, Raghu took a few deep breaths of the morning fresh air and then called Bholu to pass on the instruction.

It was probably the first time that Raghu may have woken up this early in the morning and that too in all his senses. He was totally confused about the instructions of the Boss, especially in this case. First he asked Raghu to extend him a heavy loan, then he asked Raghu to demand back the loan amount prematurely, and also asked him to get Abhi's sister followed by someone. Now suddenly he had been asked to stop following Aditi. He was totally confused about what exactly the Boss wanted him to do, or specifically, what he wanted to do with Abhi. Raghu again went to the bed and tried to sleep, but he could not. His body had woken up and was reluctant to lie down anymore. After a few minutes, he got up and went to the washroom to freshen up.

◆

Entering his cabin, Rajal first switched on the desktop, then seating himself comfortably, opened his laptop. By the time the laptop booted, the desktop was already alive and ready. Rajal ran his usual executable files on the desktop which started the job it was designed for. Several files started opening and the system started flashing data for all the tagged words. The software was tagged for certain words which if present in any of the documents was to be lined up in front in a separate folder. Rajal had given Abhi some words with which tagging was to be implemented, but then, last night Rajal had removed some words and added some other to refine the search in accordance with his needs. Checking for another one hour, Rajal did not find anything interesting for him, hence he switched his attention towards his laptop to check on his regular running projects. Focussing on his company's projects, he reviewed them on the basis of time of delivery and the level of solutions designed both on the programming part and on the user interface part.

For over four hours, Rajal was busy on his laptop, reviewing the projects and he kept noting down in his diary important points to be discussed with his team. In between, he got calls from some of his clients to apprise him of the issues that they had come across. When he felt comfortable regaining his grip back on his business, he relaxed and remembered about the work his desktop had been doing. Turning towards his desktop Rajal brought the screen to life and started checking on the latest data downloaded by the system. Grappling with the available data for over fifteen minutes, he suddenly had a tinkling in his eyes and opening the file he had a smile floating on his lips. That was it … the file opened up to a quotation document towards a project of Government of India for the installation and maintenance of a performance tracking system of the different projects handled by different departments of the government. It was a project which had low investment and high returns and whoever handled the project would automatically get projected into the big league of logistics companies.

Rajal had already started working on the solution he ought to provide and so had many other software companies. As per the government specifications, the solution was not too difficult to provide, but the maintenance of the system being of high margin attracted many players in his field. Uday Singh's Solution Informatics and Rajal's Pranam Enterprises were among the largest companies in the foray. Uday Singh somehow always got to quote less than him in all major projects and hence nearly bagged all the large projects. It was the fortress of luck around Uday Singh which Rajal planned to break into this time.

The file which made Rajal alert and attentive was related to different quotes for the jobs as was given in the original offer of document of the government. He transferred the file to a different folder and opening it from the transferred location started studying it minutely. He then turned towards his laptop and opened a file which was a quotation he had prepared based on his cost estimates. Comparing both the quotations, he could clearly see an edge in Uday Singh's quotations. He started studying all the parameters in his quotation and then began pruning certain items where he had good margins. He brought down all the important figures to as low as he thought he could afford. Preparing a fresh quotation, he again compared with that of Uday Singh's. Once again he could still see the edge in Uday's quotes. He wondered how Uday could afford this project at such low quotes. Rajal needed this job badly to foray into the big league and hence he needed to beat Uday Singh at his quotes. It was Rajal's desperation which prompted him to go for this means of hacking into Uday Singh's network and get to know about his efforts prior to the closing of quote submissions. But now after looking at the quotes, Rajal felt he could again loose if he didn't resort to price his quotation at prices much below the cost he would incur.

Rajal turned towards his laptop and started rechecking his quotation to find areas where he could further lower prices without going for a loss in the whole contract. As he deliberated on each of the items, he could see margins still generating from some parts, which he cut down. In some areas, he cut down to the cost price only with a no profit no loss situation. After lowering down his quotation figures further to the least possible, he could see that he had achieved the prices below that of Uday Singh's quotes. Once again, comparing the quotes, he was happy to see that now his quotes were slightly lower than that of his rival. With this quote, he was sure to wrest the project from Uday Singh. The quotation could not go further down. It was still a few days before closing day and he was sure he could find some more avenues of further lowering the cost.

Saving his file, he once again checked the desktop to see if any new material had arrived from Uday's closet to give him some fresh data. There was none, so he just took a printout of the quotation statement to take it home in the evening and check some data in the comfort of his own bed.

✦

Aditi felt refreshed and rejuvenated and took much interest in interacting with her students. Once again being free from the mental burden, she felt she had been reborn and was confident at being able to execute such a large job with such finesse. In between teaching her students, she went to the window twice to check if that familiar face was sitting at the tea stall on the opposite road. Finding no one, she wondered if Abhi had already settled his dues and hence the person following her must have been dropped by Raghu. She was also happy with the fact that without any extra effort, she had been able to save half the amount for herself. It was good that Abhi had also arranged for half of the amount. She thanked God and then thanked her friend's sister Alka, who had met her in the pub and advised her on how to handle men like Rajal. In her intoxicated moments, Aditi had become emotional meeting an old acquaintance in the city at an unexpected place and had shared her troubles with her. As Aditi wrapped up her work and took her bag to leave, she checked up for the change for auto rickshaw. Thats when she spotted the small bottle in the bag still more than half filled. Aditi smiled and pushed it inside the bag to be used in future.

✦

"Well bro, how is it going? Is everything fine? I haven't been able to meet you for the last couple of days. Is your project completed?"asked Shashank.

Abhi lifted his eyes from the computer screen and saw Shashank tilting on his workstation partition and said, "Yes Shashank, everything fine. By the way, I was coming to you to inform you about the progress on the section I was assigned. It is nearly complete; you start preparing for the integration of both parts. I think we can start the integration by day after tomorrow."

"That's good. I will prepare the algorithm and make it ready by tomorrow. But what about now? Are you joining us today evening for a drink?" asked Shashank.

"Yes of course, at the usual place?" enquired Abhi.

"Yes, same place. We will leave together," said Shashank and moved away to his enclosure.

Though he had promised Shashank an evening out, at the back of his mind he planned to meet Raghu and return the money he owed. After so many days, when he got an offer to loosen up, he could not resist. Since there were still some days left, he thought he could go the next morning before coming to the office and settle off his payables. Once again, checking the bag kept below his table and feeling the bundles inside it, he felt relaxed. He had brought the money with him and it was not safe to roam around the office and pub with such a large amount. Moreover, carrying it after the session at the pub and going back home through the lonely streets late night was not a wise thing to do. On second thoughts, he decided to cancel the plan and go to Raghu to pay off his debt before anything went wrong.

◆

Before leaving for the day, Rajal looked for Alka and found she had already left the office. He wanted to discuss the quotations with her, but then postponed it to the next day, when he would have deliberated on it properly and would be able to match that of Uday Singh. He had already decided to make Alka the leader of the project, hence it was necessary to discuss the quotes with her. She was the one who had to get the project operational within that cost. The areas where he was cutting costs had to be clear in Alka's mind to seamlessly run the project without cribbing. Postponing it for the next day, Rajal left for home with the quotation papers.

The day had come to an end and the birds chirped back to their nests. The sun folded its rays back to itself to allow the darkness to creep in. Slowly, the night enveloped the city, making the streets deserted, bringing the wheels to a halt.

20th Day

Rajal was re-analysing his quotations and comparing them with that of Uday Singh's when his secretary announced the arrival of Alka. He kept Uday's quotation papers in the drawer and asked Alka to be shown in.

"Good morning Boss, how are you?" greeted Alka as she entered the room.

"Good morning. I'm fine, come just check these papers," said Rajal.

Alka picked up the papers to study, "Are they the proposal papers for our bid for that government project?"

"Yes and this is my final quotation, just check the figures ... after all, you are going to handle this, so you need to be completely conversant with these figures," explained Rajal.

Looking at the documents and calculating, Alka became puzzled and recalculated all the figures. After fifteen minutes, she said frustratingly, "What is this, Boss? It is not possible to run this on such a tight budget. We cannot deliver at this price ... it's a loss proposition."

"Yes, I understand in the first go it seems so, but we have to take this chance. The profit is not in this project, but once we get to handle this, we can earn profit from other projects which may come our way due to this one," smiled Rajal.

"But at the price you have quoted, it is not possible to run this project. The amount is too little to fund our logistics. From where will we get the rest? The gap is too large," frowned Alka.

"The gap will be funded by my company to some extent, though you will not feel the fund crunch during major parts of the project. We are only quoting a lower cost to our client," explained Rajal.

"But what if we are not able to give quality work?" said Alka.

"No, no … You don't understand, the client will only pay less for a higher variant job. We are going to give the best quality and will expend extensively, but will receive only a part of it from the client … the rest will be compensated by the profit we will earn from other projects," said Rajal.

"So you are offering a predatory pricing to get this bid in your favour! But I don't think we should quote so low as none of the other bidders will be able to quote anything close to this," Alka tried to reason.

"I actually don't want to take any chances; it has to come to me … at any cost … that's why I have quoted a price which no one can afford to quote," clarified Rajal.

"As you wish. Can I have a copy of this document, so that I can plan in advance?" asked Alka.

"Yes sure. I have already got one set prepared for you as you will be heading this project."

Alka smiled and getting up holding the file said, "Is there anything left for me to plan in this? I think you have already planned it up to the last detail. I just need to ensure that we stick to that plan only. I will come back to you if I find anything more to discuss."

As the cabin door closed after Alka, Rajal again took out the papers from his drawer and once more compared figures in his document with that of Uday Singh's. He wanted to be sure to make his bid the lowest, not leaving anything to come between him and this project. After analysing the documents, he again turned the desktop on and started downloading fresh files. Running his script, he could not find anything new related to this project. Having satisfied himself, he switched off the desktop and turned towards his laptop to check if the link to submit the bids online had been activated. The bid window was of only two days and thereafter two days were reserved for analysis of all bids by the government officials. The award of the project was to be declared after that. The link had not been activated yet; it was to get activated by next day at 9:00 a.m. Rajal toggled back to his company's software to track status of his ongoing projects and check the status of complaints received from his clients.

◆

Coming back to her cabin, Alka bolted her cabin from inside and sitting down on her chair, pulled out a paper from her drawer. She kept this paper alongside the document she had brought from Rajal and started comparing them. While analysing both the documents, she had a smile floating on her lips, understanding the delicateness with which the document given to her by Rajal had been prepared.

"Rajal is smart, good work done," Alka murmured as she finished reading both the documents. Alka took out her mobile and switching on the camera clicked on the documents given by Rajal one by one. Completing the shots, she checked all the pictures on her mobile for their clarity and then gathering all the papers, kept them separately – the documents taken out from the drawer were kept in her handbag and the documents given by Rajal were kept in the drawer after properly filing them in an office folder.

In the middle of the day, Alka got a call and a lunch was fixed. Rajal had no prior appointments, hence he decided to leave for home. Abhi joined his colleagues at the office canteen. Aditi walked outside to have some tea at the roadside stall. It was a normal pleasant afternoon with no surprises. If it would not have been a working day, most of the people would have been lazing around in the afternoon sun; but it being a working day, most of the people had to return to their work as early as possible.

It was around three when Alka entered the hotel for her lunch appointment. She headed straight towards the lift lobby. As she waited for the lift, she looked around for familiar faces. She entered the lift and pressed the button for the fourth floor and headed straight to room 421.

"Hi, you are on time," she was greeted warmly by a manly hug.

"Yes and I see you have already ordered the lunch," said Alka kissing him on the cheek. "You place the plates while I freshen up. I'm so hungry," said Alka as she went towards the washroom after throwing her mobile and handbag on the bed.

In a few minutes, Alka came out only in her undergarments. She sat on the sofa and picked up her plate. For the next fifteen minutes, Alka and her date kept eating and chatting. Finishing their lunch, Alka took her partner to bed and lying down, started cuddling with him, taking out his clothes and allowing him to run his fingers on her naked body. Elongating the foreplay as the sun further moved westwards, they plunged themselves into the deep ecstasy of the satisfaction of their uninhibited carnal desires.

✦

"So, how are your stock investments? They must be pretty down," asked Shashank as he and Abhi were leaving office after a hard day's job.

"Yes, they are completely battered. No hope of recovery in the near future," replied Abhi gloomily.

"Then how will you pay back Raghu? You know these people are quite ruthless," said Shashank.

"Oh no worries, I have already repaid all ..." Abhi bit his tongue, realising he should not have disclosed this.

"Really! How? I mean from where did you get the money? As far as I know, you had placed all your savings into the stocks with the hope of recovery. So how did you manage to repay Raghu and before the due date?" said Shashank clearly surprised.

Abhi realised he had committed a blunder. It was Shashank who had introduced him to Raghu and knew that Abhi was not in a position to pay such a large amount at this point. And the kind of work they were in, it was not difficult to doubt a person's integrity towards his organisation. This matter of getting his hand on a large amount of money would make anyone suspicious. Abhi had to quickly lie to Shashank before it snowballed and the fingers started pointing towards him.

"My father gave it to me," said Abhi sheepishly and then explained further. "I was discussing it with my father over the phone and there I happened to mention about my debt and the impending fear of not being able to repay it. That is when my father became furious and asked me to settle the dues immediately. You know people of that age never want to be in debt and my father has closely watched village money lenders who extract blood out of their debtors. So he sent me the whole amount after selling one piece of his land and pursued me to pay off Raghu."

"Well, your father is a rich man!" exclaimed Shashank.

"We own agricultural land, so my father could easily arrange it," explained Abhi further.

"So if you have a kingly estate in your village, then why are you working here? You can start a business there," said Shashank.

"The land at my village is agricultural land and is located deep in the village. That land cannot be used for any commercial purpose," explained Abhi. "But yes, there is quite a large area under my family's ownership, so to make me debt free, my father offered and I simply accepted."

"Lucky man and of course a rich man. What are you doing in this petty office, Your Highness?" joked Shashank.

"Oh, come on! Life is difficult in villages and moreover, cultivation is not an easy job. I am more of a software person and not a hardware type," said Abhi.

"Okay, I understand. Let's move now. I will take your leave, see you tomorrow," Shashank said.

"But where are you going? Let's go and have some chilled beer," said Abhi holding Shashank's hand.

"No, I have some important work today and have to leave, otherwise do you think I would miss the beer party thrown by you," said Shashank laughing loudly.

"Okay, then see you tomorrow," said Abhi releasing Shashank's hand.

As Abhi went towards the waiting auto, Shashank crossed the street towards the cigarette shop. Lighting the cigarette he moved towards the deserted street round the corner and dialled Rajal from his mobile.

"Yes Shashank, how are you?" said Rajal as he picked up the call.

"Fine sir. Just wanted to confirm if your work is done, because Abhi doesn't seem to be doing anything special these days and seems quite carefree."

"Ah, yes my job is done and Abhi has done a wonderful job. You referred the correct person, he was really brilliant," confirmed Rajal.

"Yes, I knew Abhi had that special talent and I should also appreciate the patience you had in dealing with him because handling a talented person like him needs a lot of careful steps," said Shashank. "So when can I meet you ... today if you are free?" added Shashank hesitatingly.

"Well, yes you can come by. I have no special plan for today, we can have a drink together," said Rajal.

"Of course, I will come by ... and may I ask if it is the right time to tell that I may require some financial help?" said Shashank sheepishly.

"Come on Shashank! I know I have to pay you for your services and that's nothing to be so apprehensive about. I have the packet ready for you," consoled Rajal.

"Oh thank you, I am just coming. Thanks a lot", said Shashank enthusiastically and disconnecting the phone took two short puffs. Throwing away the cigarette bud, he called out for an auto.

As the elongated shadows merged into the darkness, the street lights showed the way to the blinded beings. The day came to an end with hopes for the next day preparing to take shape.

The Days After

Abhi could feel the excitement in the air as the opening bell had rung for the markets. It was after a long time that Abhi had logged into his trading account. His discussion with Shashank the previous night on his trading portfolio and the handsome amount in his bag allured him to the stock market. Another chance of recovery was in sight. He could have logged in from his home, but then leaving the market in between during opening hours could make him miss an opportunity. Glued to his monitor, the ups and downs reflected very fast as the last day's quotes, after the closing bell, took their trades. The markets rising initially fell from the last day's close in just fifteen minutes of the trading session. Some stocks seemed to be good opportunities, but past experience made Abhi restrain himself from impulsive decision taking. The previous fortnight had gradually matured Abhi to a great extent. The pause in his reaction had made a right dent in his overall disposition. He had decided just to observe the trades and not be lured into buying or selling. As he navigated into his portfolio, he could see his loss figure in red slightly improving than the last time he had checked. There must have been some upward rise in the stocks in his basket. For the next one hour, Abhi checked the trend over last fortnight for all the stocks in his portfolio. He felt there have been some days when he could have gone in for a buy which could have helped him in averaging out his total investment. But that was possible only if he had such an amount at that time. This made him realise the futility of his thinking as he himself had been nearly bankrupt.

As his other colleagues started pouring into the office, Abhi minimised the trading screen and opened his official working screen, toggling between both the screens as and when he was sure of no peeping toms around. The money involved in his portfolio was large enough for him and now that he had no obligations to pay to anyone out of this investment, he could more freely concentrate on their values instead of being in a hurry to sell at the sight of even a small profit. He now understood that he could hold on to his stocks and still keep on investing to improve the overall position. However bad the markets may be, an exit in these situations would only lead to a permanent loss, while staying on may bring recovery. Having touched rock bottom, the only way the market has is upwards; the climb may be slow but it is bound to happen. Naturally, ascent is always slower than descent. Returning back to his work, Abhi was still bewildered by his adventure of the previous fortnight. How could he execute such a risky job being a man of the desk rather than of the field, and then wondering what could be the reason for Rajal being the common factor between him and Aditi. Was it a mere coincidence or some design? Could it affect their lives in future, he wondered.

✦

Since nine in the morning, Rajal had been clicking on the link, taking his cursor till the upload option radio button, pausing there and going back. The bid uploads had started online, but Rajal was still in a dilemma whether to upload or not. He had invested too much in this project, not only what he has expended till now but what he would have to expend once he got the project. The predatory pricing has this disadvantage that it moves on a razor edge of investment and loss. It is difficult to predict when the investment will turn into a loss. Though he was sure his quotation would be the best, but still, he was in doubt about the timing of uploading his bid. Being from the IT field, he was sceptical about the security of government sites. Since this was not a site involving national security, its firewalls might not be that stringent. Even if it was secure enough, he was not sure of the honesty of the officials who would be accessing all the bids for their analysis. The window was open for two days, that is till five in the evening the next day, and two days are enough for any bidder to revise his bid. Rajal closed down the current page and returned to checking his mails. Lot of other jobs were to be handled and he had enough time to check his quotes and upload them at his own leisure.

✦

After her classes got over, Aditi summed up all the day's work and taking her handbag, went to the washroom to freshen up. She had lunch with her colleagues and came back to her lab to prepare the assignment she was going to give her students the next day. As she began, her mind started wandering towards the money she had in hand. Though she had faked her desire to start her own business of computer education while speaking to Rajal, it wasn't a bad idea. With ten lakhs in her kitty, she could start with a small venture. But no matter how small it'd be, it will be her own venture and she would be free from the clutches of the rules laid down by others. An environment created by her for herself would be more comfortable than working for someone else on a fixed salary. But again, self-created setups had their own risks; it is not only profits but losses also which need to be borne. In a job for others, at least you have a security of a fixed salary every month; but in an entrepreneurship venture, the erratic nature of expendable income was quite intimidating. What if she was not able to find enough students? What if the fee structure was not able to completely fund the infrastructure cost like rent of premises, cost of computers, internet connectivity, latest software, teachers' salaries, the accreditation fees and other such expenses? Would it be easy for her to run an institute? She had been more comfortable in a fixed time salaried job. Her mind wandered towards Rajal and the thought that kept striking her was how had Rajal emerged as the common factor between her and Abhi? Was it a coincidence or had someone designed it purposely?

The canteen was bursting with fun and cheer as Shashank had ordered pizzas for everyone. Abhi was also enjoying the fun with everyone, but was unable to understand the reason for the pizza party. Everyone was surprised when they asked Shashank to give a party just for fun and he instantly agreed to it. Shashank had been one of the jolly fellows in the group, but he seemed to be in quite a jovial mood, as if walking on air that day. Shashank came up to Abhi with a pizza box and handing it to him said, "Here, have it, it's specially for you."

"Specially for me? Why? Have I done something that you are showering this bounty on me?" laughed Abhi.

"Yes of course, you are the reason for this party," said Shashank smiling.

"How? What have I done?"

"Well you are my best friend. I have no family member to share my good or bad moods, so I share it with you," replied Shashank.

"And may I know the reason behind your good mood?" enquired Abhi.

"Well lend me thy ears, my friend," whispered Shashank and then closing towards Abhi's ears, whispered, "I think I will be able to leave this job soon and start my own venture. Things are falling into place."

"Wow, good! So you are going to be the next Uday Singh, please do remember petty people like us … we may also be of some use to Your Highness," said Abhi bowing.

Amused, Shashank also said "Of course my dear subject, you are a very important brick in my venture. How can I forget you? You will be granted the position of an important courtesan in my court," said Shashank placing his right palm over Abhi's head and then laughed out loudly. Abhi held Shashank's hand and pulled him in a hug, whispering in his ear, "I am proud of you, my friend; you are on path of making your own mark." Shashank had a smile on his face while embracing him and thanking Abhi from inside for being able to pull off Rajal's job successfully which had made Shashank richer by five lakhs overnight.

✦

Raghu dialled the number stored on his mobile in the name of 'Boss'. He needed to discuss on the money returned by Abhi the day before. As Raghu apprised him of the money received, he was instructed to deposit it in his bank account, details of which were already available with Raghu. Having received the instructions clearly, Raghu disconnected the call.

On the other side, 'Boss' Rajal had a smile floating on his lips on the way he had orchestrated the whole affair. Destiny gave him a chance to hit two targets with a single bullet and his well-planned moves ensured that he got successful in the same. He still remembered how in order to make a dent in Uday Singh's company, he had come across Shashank who as his informers had told him, was one of the best hackers and a vulnerable person looking at his expenditure pattern and his ambitions in life. He had offered a good amount to Shashank to convert him into his mole in Uday Singh's organisation, which Shashank readily accepted, but expressed his inefficiency in breaking into the organisation's systems and suggested Abhi's name as an expert who could perform the feat. But he was also warned that Abhi wouldn't turn against his organisation just for the money and would have to be lured indirectly.

As usual, before embarking on a new project Rajal always did a pre-check on his target and hence got a discreet enquiry done on Abhi. That is where he came to know that he was the brother of Aditi, whom he had longed for so long. Abhi's interest towards expensive and branded items and his latest obsession with stock markets gave him a chance to utilise it as an opportunity. Rajal had been a good stock market man and his wit had warned him of bumpy days ahead. According to him, the markets had reached a zenith and close to a drastic correction, hence sanely, he withdrew most of his investments from the market. But with the help of Shashank, he lured Abhi to borrow from Raghu, who readily obliged being financed by Rajal. Raghu had been his old man whom he had helped escape the clutches of the law and in return had utilised his services. He now didn't need Raghu much for those jobs since his small firm has transformed into a large corporate and the competition was large enough to get intimidated by small henchmen like Raghu.

Rajal financed Abhi through Raghu at the right time and through Shashank ensured that Abhi invested all this money into stocks. Thereafter, he patiently waited for a few months when the stock market came crashing down to such levels that there was no recovery possible and that was the time he asked Raghu to hit at Abhi with an instant demand of the loan. He also ensured that Raghu hit Abhi in the complete knowledge of his sister Aditi in a way that it would be difficult for Aditi to escape Rajal's clutches.

During his profiling of Abhi, Rajal had already become aware that the relationship between both siblings was such that they would try to help each other. There were certain assumptions on which Rajal depended and luckily they all fell into place. It helped him to trap Abhi to do his job as well as make Aditi fall into his lap. Though it was a different story that the Aditi episode had not turned out as well as expected, but then, that was an extra advantage that he wanted to derive. The Abhi episode had worked quite successfully and he was just a few days away from his grand success. Though he just got twenty lakhs back, money had never been a proposition in this game; it had just acted as a conduit. Rajal stretched back on his chair with both hands at the back of his head and murmured, "I feel like God. I have made things happen my way and now will taste success my way … yeah … I am God."

✦

"I think we need to be more open and talk in detail about the coincidence of Rajal in our lives. I think it's important for us to come out openly with this Rajal factor," said Aditi at the breakfast table along with Abhi. Aditi was having a bad feeling about the whole coincidence, since coincidences are very rare in real life.

"You have just put words to my thoughts," said Abhi. "How is it that we both approached the same man and got exactly what we required?"

"Exactly what we required? But you said you arranged only half the amount," said Aditi.

"I didn't tell you, but I arranged the complete amount through Rajal only," said Abhi sheepishly.

"So you lied to me."

"No, I didn't lie, I just didn't tell you. I simply used half of what both of us earned and left half for us for our own individual use," explained Abhi.

"Okay, let's push it back and come to the point as to how we both approached the same person. This seems strange. I have known him for the last couple of years and had approached him since I knew he was the only person in my circle who could help with this kind of amount. But how did you contact him?"

"Through an advertisement where he required some freelancer. When I approached him and told him my requirement, he offered me an assignment, so I entered into a deal with him", said Abhi.

"So we both had separate deals but nearly at the same time and with the same person. In this big city, why did we get to have a deal with same person at same time and also for the same purpose?" Aditi deliberated.

"I am also quite clueless on this strange coincidence, but giving thought to it at length, I am also not able to establish any relationship in the whole transaction," said Abhi.

"The problem came to me, I didn't tell you … but you came to know because you overheard us and you started your own efforts independently while I went my own different way. So there doesn't seem to be any other explanation apart from it being a coincidence."

"True, and I can't press my brain to think harder. Let's finish our breakfast and leave," saying that, Aditi got up and went to the kitchen to wash her plate. She needed to run for the office, and Abhi followed suit.

✦

Alka entered Rajal's cabin and wishing him for the day sat across him. "So have we bid or are you still thinking of some revision in the quotes?"

"Yes we are bidding with the same quotes, but of course we have time till five. I don't want to upload my application at a time when there is still time for others to revise their quotes," said Rajal.

"Do you still think someone will be able to quote even lower? I was expecting an upward revision," said Alka.

"Upward revision! No way, this is the highest I can go if I have to get this project," said Rajal.

"Are you sure we can handle this loss? The project is big and will be under our maintenance for quite a few years".

"It is not loss, it is negative profit; and we will offset this negative profit against a larger profit that I expect sooner. When we start getting other projects, I plan to have a separate book prepared to keep track of the actual profit we make offsetting with this negative profit," explained Rajal in detail.

"I don't know what to say, but somehow I am not feeling comfortable," said Alka, reluctance apparent on her face.

"You are not feeling comfortable since you are not able to envision the larger picture. Sometimes to take a long stride ahead, you need to first take two steps back, to generate that recoil which will push you forward with astronomical pace," explained Rajal enthusiastically.

"How are you so confident that we will get bigger projects after this?"

"The technicalities involved in this project will develop a different skill set, required for handling other such projects and clients will look forward to engage us, the experienced guys. This project is just to develop this comfort in our prospective clients," Rajal once again explained in detail.

"And you are also sure no one will be able to quote the rates below us with all the other offerings?"

"Of course I am sure, why would I have even gone so far if I had any such doubt? There is a lot at stake now and a lot of planning and preparations have gone into the same," said Rajal "You see, I have been preparing for this for over six months now".

"Six months! But this project was declared only a month back."

"My planning had not been this project specific, but it was in general, to beat the competition. When this project came by a month ago, I just gave speed to my preparations and put it in execution mode. That is why I was able to come up with a quote which no one can beat ... simply no one," said Rajal confidently.

"But aren't you forgetting Uday Singh's Solution Informatics? They have always been able to beat us in high status project bids, though this time I think Uday Singh will not be able to match your figure unless he gives it for free," jeered Alka.

"Yes, this time he will have to give it for free to beat me, but don't worry, I have taken special care of him this time. He just can't beat me this time," said Rajal dauntlessly.

"What is that special arrangement you have done this time?"

"Nothing special, but you can say whatever he does will be under my watch. I will tell you once we are through with this deal," said Rajal.

"Fine then, I will leave now and if there is any change in the quotes, please do let me know," said Alka as she got up.

"I will," said Rajal.

Rajal switched on the desktop to check for any latest download from Uday Singh's laptop. He didn't find anything of much interest except that Uday Singh was busy reviewing his ongoing projects. Would that mean that Uday Singh had already finalised his quote and was not revising it anymore? Was he so confident on his quotes that he didn't need any revisions? But yes, why would he require any revisions, he had already prepared the quotes at such low rates, that if Rajal had not seen it he could not have prepared a better quote. In a world of competition, you cannot always win thinking straight and this time you will get a lesson Mister Uday, thinking aloud Rajal cajoled himself smilingly. In just a few hours, he would upload his bid, leaving no scope for any of the other bidders.

✦

Uday Singh was sitting in his cabin and reviewing his other projects when he got a call on his mobile, while he was listening to the call he sensed another call on waiting, it was from his general manager operations. He politely disconnected the first call and connected to his GM. He had called to remind him that they needed to upload their bid for the government project. There were only two hours left for the window to close. Uday Singh checked the time and asked his GM to come to him after thirty minutes and take the hard copy from him to upload on the link from his own system. Uday Singh realised that of late his system had become slow, maybe after that fall in the lift, some hardware part was not functioning correctly and hence slowing down the processing speed. Moreover, he had already discussed the final quotes with his GM and let him upload the quotation as always. Whatever final corrections were required he had done on the hard copy in the form of his noting which his GM could easily understand and upload accordingly. As per the phone call he was engaged in before, the quotes as finalised by him would have to remain same and it made him confident.

✦

Aditi checked several sites on the net to get an insight into establishing her computer teaching institute. She checked the formalities required to start a new venture with respect to registration and the minimum requirement. She also checked the different franchisee offers floating on the net. But franchisee offers required greater investments and starting afresh had so many other formalities that it seemed the available money would be completely exhausted even before she was able to take the first admission. It seemed another twenty lakhs would be required to ultimately start her venture. Rajal was not an option for her now. She wondered if she should she go for another target and repeat her feat again? Would'nt that be easier this time? Oh my God! What was she thinking; it was not only dangerous but highly unethical. Was the dream of having her institute taking over her senses? But what was the harm if people were ready to be fooled themselves. No one was getting hurt; it was just a deal where mutual requirements were settled without any remorse. It was a good idea though; the question was how to find a target, and how to go about searching for the right person.

✦

It was around 4:40 p.m. when Rajal uploaded his bid and as the screen extended thanks for showing interest in the project, Rajal relaxed on his chair. He had to wait for two days to get this project awarded to his company and thereafter get his team to complete this project in record time. As Rajal was planning ahead the steps towards successful completion of the project, another bid got uploaded from another system at Solution Informatics. The two biggest companies had uploaded their bids, each confident of their own terms. Finally the link closed down at five, taking in some more last minute bids from some other bidders.

✦

Abhi had so far restrained from going for any deal on the market, but by the end of the day's session he became too restless to control himself. One of the stocks he had been tracking had fallen down to its fifty-two week low and was tempting him with the strong fundamentals the company had and how it can perform much better looking at its credentials. That day the company had got a beating due to excessive pressure from FIIs but it should rebound very soon. This was a great opportunity for Abhi to plunge into the markets again and hold this stock for some time. With a conflicting state of mind, Abhi finally put in a bid of his own for just one lakh rupees after the close of the session to be able to get benefit of the morning bell the next day. After having put in his bid, Abhi felt a lot of weight releasing out of his head which he had been carrying. It was very difficult for him to neither invest in the market nor buy some new gadget with so much of money in his hands. The urge to spend is difficult to control, especially when it has been a long time since one has done any shopping. But then after having once again invested and having watched the market perform over the last two days, Abhi got some more notions. Why not invest heavily in the market at this time, it was the best time to put in money and get hold of some premium stocks at rock bottom prices. This tactic could make him earn large amounts.

But then he would have to first arrange for a method to show his money as legal with all taxes paid. He needed to figure out a way to place his money through banking channels and then route them to the stock market. What's wrong in earning more money from people who are always in search of freelancers like him. If he could pull off such a dangerous job involving hard coding, he was prepared for hacking jobs in the software field itself. There is much of corporate spying going on and his skills will be much in demand.

✦

These were busy times. Abhi had been spending the last two days searching for people who might be interested in his skills. Aditi had been busy studying people in a particular income bracket who might be interested in *her* skills. The last twenty days had evolved two relatively good persons into hunting vultures ready to grasp their prey as soon as they sight them. This was called evolution of species and development of the world as a whole.

✦

Rajal got ready early in the morning as he had to reach the office of the Department of Planning and Supervision by ten when the quotations were to be made public and award of the project was to be declared. He had to pick up Alka to take her along. It was a big event for Rajal. It was the first time that he was this close to beating his biggest rival. As he reached Alka's house, Alka came running out, equally excited.

As they reached the designated hall, it was already half filled with representatives of the firms and companies who had bid for the project. As Rajal and Alka entered, they could straight away sight Uday Singh and his general manager sitting across the hall in the front row. Both of them approached Uday Singh and had formal greetings exchanged. This time Rajal showed more confidence with respect to his earlier interactions.

The meeting started exactly at 10:10 a.m. After initial introductions, proclamations and disclaimers, the official who was to deliver the result took the podium.

"A very good morning to all of you. As you all already know the importance of this project for the government and other details as just now explained by Secretary sir, we had invited bids to award this project to a company who can prepare and maintain this programme over the next twenty years with minimum cost and maximum efficiency. We were pleased to get a very high number of bids and on analysis of these bids found that there are so many companies in our country that can carry on this programme with not only keeping the cost under control but also with a very high degree of quality. Out of the total thirty-five bids received, our committee shortlisted ten and then further analysed them. These ten bids which were shortlisted were on the basis of their earlier experiences on projects handled, their commitment on time of completion, the add-on services which they were offering and of course the cost effectiveness. These ten bids were thoroughly analysed by our technical evaluation team and by our planning team. Out of these ten bids, we narrowed down to three bids which were offering similar services and had offered nearly the same time of completion of the project. These three bids were then sorted out on the basis of the cost structures they were offering and the bid which had the lowest cost was accepted to be awarded this project."

Rajal looked at Alka and as Alka looked towards Rajal, she could spot tiny drops of sweat on his forehead. She gently put her hand on Rajal's and pressed it softly to reassure him.

"I would now name the three companies whose bids were shortlisted for the final decision. These companies are Pranam Enterprises ..."

Rajal had a smile on his face and turning up his palm held Alka's hand tightly.

"... Solution Informatics ..."

Uday Singh looked towards Rajal and exchanged smiles.

"... and Samadhan Infosolutions ..."

Rajal had already started feeling the punch in his stomach and was just waiting for the final name to be disclosed. No other company except Uday Singh's Solution Informatics and his Pranam Enterprises was capable enough to give such low quotes and since he had already bettered Solution Informatics, it was just a matter of seconds now that he would get the project.

"All these three companies have offered nearly similar services and committed nearly equal time for completion of the project. Even on the cost front, these three companies are neck to neck and the lowest price quoted among the three, who is also awarded the project is ... Samadhan Infosolutions."

"What! Samadhan ... how could it be ... but how could it be ..." said Rajal, hysterically looking at Alka in total disbelief. "It is impossible! A company which is much younger, how can it offer a quote better than me ... it is impossible!" muttered Rajal.

"Calm down ... listen, just calm down," saying Alka tightening her grip on Rajal's hand. She forcefully tried to control him, while the announcement continued.

"While we congratulate Samadhan Infosolutions for bagging the project and welcome them on board, we would also like to congratulate Pranam Enterprises for being the second best and Solution Informatics for being the third best among the total thirty-five bids received by us."

"The third best!" exclaimed Alka astonished and releasing Rajal's hand turned her eyes towards Uday Singh questioning him. Uday Singh also looked at Alka with a smile on his face and gestured Alka to calm down. While Rajal sat still numb in disbelief, he did not notice the silent conversation between Alka and Uday Singh.

"The third best!" Alka again murmured not able to understand why Uday Singh hadn't revised his quotation to make it better than Rajal's even after she had passed on the bid document of Rajal's bid to him. After the momentary shock, Alka immediately gathered herself and saw Rajal holding his head in both of his hands, close to a breakdown.

"Well ladies and gentlemen, we thank you for participating in the bid and look forward to working with you in the future." The announcer finished his presentation and this was also the sign for all the guests to get up and start moving. But Rajal was not moving at all and just remained seated, holding his head in his palms. As Uday Singh approached Alka and Rajal, Alka shook Rajal and brought him back to his senses gesturing towards Uday Singh, who was standing in front of him extending his hand. Rajal got up and shaking hands with Uday Singh said, "Bad luck. I think someone else had better resources than us."

"Yeah, may be ... but don't lose heart. The world doesn't end here, we will meet somewhere else and I congratulate you for your bid being better than mine. Well, see you then and best wishes." Saying so, Uday Singh shook hands with Rajal and then slowly extended his hand towards Alka, "And a very good day to you, Miss Alka."

"Good day to you too, sir," replied Alka as she separated her hand and felt a piece of paper stuck in her palm.

As Rajal also started moving towards the exit door, Alka following him surreptitiously read the words on the sticky paper in her palm which read, 'Room 421, today 3:30 p.m.' She sneaked a peek at Uday Singh who turned his head slightly back and winked at Alka.

It was noon and instead of being busy with his daily project reviews, Rajal was lying on the couch in his cabin, staring at the ceiling. Alka was also sitting on the opposite sofa with her chin over her palm and looking at Rajal. She had already known that Rajal wouldn't get the contract, but was not prepared for the turn of events that took place that morning. She could see the gloom on Rajal's face, but the same was not visible on Uday's. She had ensured that Uday got the latest figures of Rajal's bid, but still Uday couldn't make it better. Was Uday not ready to bear the loss in the project or did he make some mistake in preparing his quotation? If that was a mistake, it was grave; and if it was the incapacity to run the project at a loss, then it was Uday's call. But how come a young company like Samadhan could quote such a low price?

"I think you should get over it now … at least your arch rival couldn't better you this time,"said Alka breaching the silence of the room. Rajal didn't respond and just kept his eyes stuck on the ceiling.

"Come on Rajal … it's over, let's move on. There are other projects that we need to concentrate upon. You are a businessman and these setbacks do take place, but that doesn't mean we remain glued to them. We should also see the positives, like you have now been able to break the jinx of not getting better than Uday Singh's quotes. This time you were better than him," said Alka.

"Shut up," barked Rajal. "This time this project was mine, except that bloody organisation coming out of nowhere and snatching the bite. Someone has snatched the bite from my mouth ... it could not have been Uday Singh and that I had already ensured," said Rajal growling.

"Already ensured? Means you knew Uday Singh wouldn't be able to beat you, but how? Did you have a deal with someone in the government department?" asked Alka startled at this new disclosure.

"Are you a fool? If I had had a deal with someone in the department, then the contract would have been mine. Why the hell would it have gone to anyone else?" yelled Rajal.

"I was trying to reason out ..."

"Please don't ... and leave me alone, we will talk tomorrow ..." saying that, Rajal gestured her to go out.

Alka immediately got up and looking at the clock once again, she walked out speedily.

✦

As Alka ventured out of the lift on the fourth floor of the hotel, she again checked her watch; it was nearly three. Entering room 421, she locked the door from inside and yelled, "What was that Uday? You had his figures, still you chose to lose? What the hell is going on and from where has this Samadhan come into the picture?"

"Sit down and have some coffee, I will explain. As for Samadhan, I am myself clueless, but yes for Rajal, I chose to lose. I knew it was a good project but after looking at Rajal's figures, I knew he was dealing a loss proposition. He might have been doing it in expectation of future profits, but it was too big a risk for my capacity. Hence I chose to lose it, but lose it with dignity and also I wanted Rajal to get this project at the price he had quoted. It would have made a large dent in his finances and that would have given me space to further hit him by bagging many other large projects which his finances would not have allowed him to grab. Leaving this project to Rajal was my one step backward to generate the recoil energy. Do you understand now ... it was actually a win for me if Rajal would have got this project. But Samadhan Infosolutions has made me lose. This was a blow for which I was not prepared," explained Uday Singh in detail.

"But then, this time my efforts were in vain, which means I lose my part too," said Alka.

"No my dear, your job has been to bring information, for which I pay you and you have done your job. You will get the payment. What I do with that information is my purview and that cost will be borne by me," said Uday.

"So that means I am still in business."

"Yes you are, and I think we have the whole afternoon to enjoy the swings of our businesses," said Uday smiling and closing in on Alka.

"Well then why let this afternoon pass away? Let's make it a day," saying Alka loosened Uday's tie knot and clicked open his neck button. Soon, both of them were entangled with each other in bed, forgetting the swings of their businesses and engrossed in swings of an eternal bliss.

◆

There had been many calls received all through the day congratulating him for bagging the prestigious project. In the evening when the phone rang again, he picked up the call. "Hello, Samadhan Infosolutions. How may I help you?"

"Is it Mr Sanjeev Chopra?"

"Yes, Sanjeev Chopra from Samadhan Infosolutions. May I know who I am talking to?"

"Hi, Mr Sanjeev. This is Rajal from Pranam Enterprises. First let me congratulate you for the well-deserved project, my best wishes."

"Ah thanks Mr Rajal, thanks for the wishes," reciprocated Sanjeev.

"It was a great day for you, but I am still surprised at how you'll be able to execute the project with such low pricing," said Rajal.

"Same as you must have planned it out. I checked your bid too; it was quite low," replied Sanjeev.

"Yeah, my quote was quite low, but I had the capacity to bear the shock, yours is a comparatively new firm ... it may not be able to bear this shock. If you require any collaboration, I am open to it and we can discuss the same openly," said Rajal offering a collaboration from his company.

"I appreciate your concern Mr Rajal, but rest assured, my company is completely geared up to handle this project alone. Thanks for your offer, I will keep it in mind for the bigger projects that we may come across" replied Sanjeev politely.

"Well, as you wish. My best wishes again and see you soon."

"Thanks and see you soon," disconnecting the call, Sanjeev smiled looking at his phone and then looked across the table at his guest and said, "It seems Rajal is pissed off and wants a back door entry to this project".

"Yes, he is bound to feel that way. After all, had planned and invested a lot to get this project, and you know I have also benefitted from it. He had paid five lakhs to me too in hard cash," saying that Shashank laughed out loudly at imagining the facial expression of Rajal.

"I also feel bad as I had also done my bit. I had given him Abhi who ensured that Rajal beat Uday Singh, but then life has so many unexpected turns, one should be more careful," mocked Shashank.

◆

By six, Uday Singh was driving back to his office, still intoxicated with Alka's smell. She had been a really enchanting lady and highly professional also. Had she not been so professional, he might have had to pay less for all the information she had been providing, but she always kept business and pleasure separate. It seemed pleasure was what she took for herself without incurring any cost. For the last five years, every large project had been coming to Uday Singh, and it was thanks to Alka, who always gave away Rajal's key points on time. For other smaller projects, Uday Singh never cared and always quoted higher, even after knowing Rajal's bids. This ensured no other competitor emerged as Rajal's firm remained good in business by bagging nearly all such smaller projects while Uday Singh managed larger cases. But keeping a mole in the competitor's company always had its own risks. It was better to use it sparingly. Uday Singh's excellent business acumen always signalled him to limit using Alka's services.

While turning towards his office building, Uday Singh didn't enter his building; instead, he drove ahead and crossing four more buildings, entered the fifth building and parked the car in the parking. Taking the lift, he went to the eighth floor and passing through many office doors, knocked at one of the doors. In just about a few seconds, the door opened and he was let in. Uday Singh entered the hall which comprised several workstations and enclosures. Three or four persons were glued to their desktops or laptops, busy with their work. Rest of the workstations were empty and it seemed they were never occupied by anyone. The office seemed to be a new set-up and did not employ many employees. At the far end was a door which opened into a cabin comprising a large table with a plush chair, along with leather chairs for visitors and a sofa set on one side. As Uday Singh entered the cabin, Sanjeev and Shashank immediately got up and wished him,

"Welcome, Boss. What took you so long?"

"I had some other important deals to take care of, so how do you plan to go ahead now?" asked Uday.

"As you guide us. We have been going along as you suggested and since we are in middle of it now, we have to start the work."

"Well then Sanjeev, as I had already assured you of the funds, you start the project as per your quotations and then complete the same on time. Also make sure that you get enough clout so that you get as many projects as you can. This project was lucrative for the reason that whichever company executes this project will get projected as a company that can manage large projects and hence will invite many others," said Uday Singh.

"But Boss, I still don't understand one thing. When you could have got the project yourself in your own company's name, then why did you use this company of yours to get this project?" questioned Shashank, seemingly bewildered by all this arrangement.

"You are too naive to understand this. Everything is for a purpose and whenever that time comes, the purpose gets fulfilled. I had floated this company Samadhan Infosolutions – just another name of Solution Informatics – to use it when the time comes. This was the time; a big government project like this is the correct time to launch the company in the big league. For years I have been running this company through Sanjeev with small assignments as I wanted to develop one more company in the market to take on the competition. In future, it is possible that some of my competitors may try to break the monopoly of Solution Informatics and become successful. Then I have this company Samadhan Infosolutions as a back up. It's a business game, you won't understand it easily. Now Shashank, I assign you, along with Sanjeev to join this company and help him complete the project," saying that Uday Singh got up to leave, then turning around said, "And no one, simply no one should ever come to know that I am the true owner of this company. The veil cannot be lifted at any cost ... till the correct time arrives."

"Yes Boss. I understand," said Sanjeev and came forward to open the door. Shashank also came up and asked, "But Boss what about Abhi? Is he also in with us?"

"No, he is not in the team. His job is over and we have paid him accordingly, no more than that," saying that, Uday Singh left the cabin and moved out of office.

While taking out his car from the parking, he remembered how in one of the deals, Alka had increased her price and had indirectly threatened to stop passing information if her price was not met. That one incident had forced Uday Singh to think of an alternative. That is when he remembered the evening when he was sitting behind Rajal's table during dinner at that conclave of software companies. There he had seen Rajal rebuked by a lady who was a stunning beauty. As by his nature Uday Singh had seen every event as an opportunity, he got his driver to get complete details of Aditi. Thereafter, he had got her brother appointed with him and gave him enough exposure towards hacking techniques. Abhi had also impressed him with his talent and soon became a good choice for his next move.

Uday Singh while driving back to his office building patted himself on making Shashank convince Rajal on getting Abhi on board. Uday knew Rajal would prefer Abhi because of Aditi and would create a situation where Abhi had to do things Rajal's way. And when Shashank told him that Rajal had got Abhi on board, Uday Singh had to just wait for Abhi's moves. The day Abhi met him in the lift and his laptop fell from his hand, he knew the time had come. His move was next. That is why as Abhi left Uday Singh's cabin after repairing it, he immediately got it checked by Shashank who instantly identified the bug placed in his laptop.

Uday Singh parked his car and went up the lift to his cabin. By the time he reached his cabin, it was already eight and most of the staff had already left. He dialled at Abhi's workstation and called him to his cabin. Abhi was waiting for him as Uday had already informed him to stay back.

In a few minutes, Abhi knocked the door and came into the cabin.

"You wanted to talk to me, Boss," said Abhi.

"Yes Abhi, take a seat," Uday gestured towards the visitor's chair which was immediately occupied by Abhi. "I wanted to thank you for what you have done; it really worked absolutely as designed."

Nervously, Abhi said, "Thank you sir, and I am still feeling guilty for what I did. But please understand my situation, I had to do it."

"Oh forget it, it's a business world; there is nothing to be guilty of. You did what seemed right to you. And you were so perfect … I am proud of your talent. Had I not accidentally discovered it you might not have had to face such guilty position, but leave it now. I am grateful for the way you reverse planted Rajal's laptop for me. Now I can check real time what Rajal is doing on his laptop. I have tested it on the recent project tenders. The data given to me by my source tallied exactly with what I had retrieved from the desktop set up in my office by you as a remote mirror device of Rajal's system," said Uday Singh in one long monologue.

"I offered you ten lakhs which I now fulfil and expect that in future, you will use your talent in my favour and not against me," continuing, Uday Singh took out a packet from his drawer and handed it to Abhi.

Abhi got up, held the packet and said, "Sir, it will never happen again and I am thankful to you to have condoned my fallacy. I will not give you any opportunity in future to point fingers at me," saying that, Abhi left the cabin.

There was no need for Uday to tell Abhi that he had been manipulated to commit the treacherous act by Uday himself. Catching him red-handed, Uday compelled him to plant a similar bug into Rajal's laptop. Abhi agreed to the same and by the time he prepared another set of instruments, Uday had got transferred his mailbox and other important files to a separate system with the help of Abhi, leaving some regular and unimportant items on his old laptop to enable Rajal to access them at his will. He left it to Abhi to plan how he would install the same in Rajal's system. But yes, when he completed the act, Uday could clearly check Rajal's activities through the desktop in his office. He cross checked the quotation figures as on Rajal's system and what Alka had provided him; they both tallied figure by figure. This eliminated the complete dependency on Alka for all the information, but he had to keep Alka also active since there was some information out of the system which he needed to remain updated about. Uday Singh also let Rajal track his laptop so that he could feed him information that he'd want Rajal to know.

◆

It was again pay day for Abhi and as he entered his flat, he saw Aditi at the dining table savouring a hot and delicious pizza. Abhi went to his room and freshening up hurried to the dining table to have the bite from his portion. They chatted away as they ate. Aditi then proposed whether they could both take leave from their offices and visit their parents, to which Abhi readily agreed. Finishing their dinner, they both sat down to watch television and after half an hour, Abhi bid Aditi goodnight and retired to his room. Locking his room from inside, Abhi first checked the packet given by Uday Singh which contained packets of five hundred rupee notes. Stacking them deep inside his almirah, Abhi climbed into his bed, taking his partly read book along and started turning the pages. He also flip opened the screen of the laptop and switched it on. While the laptop completed the boot sequence, he turned a few leaves of the book and keeping the book back on the table, reached for his bag. From his bag he took out another screen which he had bought from the electronics market under the seconds sale. Connecting this screen also to his laptop, he connected to the internet and after punching in a few commands, the system started processing and providing output on both screens. As Abhi looked at one screen, it had the heading 'Rajal's Screen' and on the other screen was flashing 'Uday's Screen'. He started the download from both screens and then searched for some keywords to test whether both the systems gave proper search results.

"Bingo!" muttered Abhi and patted himself to be able to access the key decision making systems of the two major companies in his field. When Abhi had fixed another laptop of Uday's and transferred data, Abhi had installed his much more modified and further miniaturised tracking bug which now showed Uday's actual laptop's events on his second screen. He was now the seller of important information of both the companies to whoever needed it and was ready to pay. He already knew some of the companies in the market who would readily be his prospective buyers.

"Both of them used me for their convenience, but did they think I have no brains? Poor guys … do they really think they are smarter than me," muttered Abhi, closing down the system, and switching off the lights.

The night thus goes by,
Making way for the morning light,
Sleep like dead in your isles,
Wake up fresh, active and alight,
Thus goes life,
A ray of light showing
After every dark night.